Nightmare by Francis Stevens

A pseudonym of Gertrude Barrows Bennett

Gertrude Barrows Bennett was born in Minneapolis on 18th September 1884.

She completed school up to the eighth grade, then switched to night school to study illustration, unfortunately she was never able to achieve a career in this. As a fall-back she began working as a stenographer, a career which she would keep to for the rest of her life.

But Gertrude had talent, writer's talent. Her first short story was written when she was 17. Not you would think the usual subjects of curious teenage girls with headstrong ambitions but a science fiction story entitled 'The Curious Experience of Thomas Dunbar'. She mailed the finished story to Argosy, one of the most well known of the pulp magazines. The story was published in the March 1904 issue.

Whilst her career was to be short and not at all prolific she is best remembered for her excellent ideas, many of which were way ahead of their time. By the time of her death in 1948 her pseudonym of 'Francis Stevens' could lay claim to being a respected and much admired author of science fiction and dark fantasy short stories and novels.

Index of Contents

CHAPTER I

"Philip, did you notice that tall, thin man in the gray ulster, who was walking up and down the boat-deck just before dinner?"

"Yes, sir. I observed the gentleman. Very haristocratic appearance, if I may say so, Mr. Jones."

"Exactly. He never bought that ulster in New York. When we reach London I want you to look around and see if you can find a tailor who will make me one of the same cut."

"Very well, sir. Very good taste, if I may say so, Mr. Jones."

"You may. And—let's see—I need a few new golf sticks, and—a dozen new shirts. Why did you pack this automatic in this trunk, Philip? Put it in that suitcase."

"Yes, sir. I 'ardly thought you'd require it while on board the Lusitania, Sir, if I may say so, Mr. Jones."

"Certainly you may. No, events requiring a pistol as stage-property are not frequent on a liner. By the way, you never showed me how to work the thing, Philip."

"No, Sir. The shopman from whom I purchased it declared it simple of hoperation, but I 'ave not found it so sir."

"Well, find out in London and show me. I never met a burglar, but if I ever should it would be embarrassing to point a pistol at him and not be able to fire it off. I admire the heroes of burglar stories. They're always such efficient people."

"Hunder exciting circumstances, sir, one becomes much more efficient. They bring it out of a man, if I may say so, Mr. Jones."

"By all means. Well, golf is exciting enough for me. Merridale and I are going to run over to the St. Andrews links. It's been the dream of my life to play the St. Andrews, but something has always come up to prevent."

"Nothing is likely to hoccur, I am sure, sir. Shall I repack the steamer trunk now, Mr. Jones?"

"Yes. And call me a little earlier, in the morning, Philip. I have an idea it's going to be fine weather, and since it's the last of the voyage I want to make the most of it. What time is it? Eleven, eh? Well, I'll go to bed early for once and get a good night's rest. Thank Heaven for a quiet life, Philip. Cribbage and the Times for you, golf and—"

"Beg pardon for hinterrupting, sir, but do you want this book packed in the trunk?"

"'Paradise Island'? Yes, pack the thing away. Did you ever read it, Philip?"

"No, sir. I don't care for them himpossible stories, if I may say so, sir."

"And welcome. Now, I'm thirty-two years old, I've yachted, ridden, motored and been about the world a good bit, and I've never had a real adventure in my life. People don't have adventures unless they're gentlemen in the filibustering line, or polar explorers, or something like that. This modern world of ours is as safe as a church, barring accidents, and they are never romantic. End in a hospital or a beastly morgue. Anybody I suppose, can find trouble by looking for it, but that's not exactly in my line."

"No, sir. Very bad form, sir, if I may say so, Mr. Jones."

"You may indeed. Here, I'll help you with that strap, and then—bed."

Ragged fragments of cloud raced across a sky where great, brilliant stars beamed fitfully. The wind hurled the wave crests through space, so that the air was almost as watery as the wide waste of billows and creaming surges in the midst of which Mr. Roland C. Jones, of New York City, found himself most unexpectedly struggling.

How it could be that he was here battling for his life, with the stars, the wind and raging, tumbling seas for his sole companions, did not immediately trouble him. He was too thoroughly engaged in trying to get a breath that was not half or all salt water to concern himself about either past or future. The mere physical present was a little bit more than he could comfortably handle.

But the fight between man and sea was too unequal. Mr. Jones was a fair swimmer, but not being provided with gills he found it impossible to get a living modicum of oxygen out of the saturated air, even when the waves did not go clean over his head. Thoroughly exhausted, more than half drowned, he had just decided that he might as well throw up his arms and let the sea have its will of him, when he found himself rising upon the shoulder of a particularly mighty billow.

For an instant he caught a glimpse of something dark and huge looming above him. Then he was in the trough again, but only for a moment. Up, up he was borne in a long, swift, surging motion. The water seemed to fall away from under him. He was on his knees in sand and the receding breaker was trying to drag him back with it. The next wave, however, carried him much farther up the beach, dropping him with a vicious thud when it was done with him.

Barely conscious of his own efforts, Jones dragged himself along on hands and knees until he was actually out of reach of the ocean which had been so unappreciative as to spew him up.

For a time he lay still, gasping the water out of lungs and stomach, then rolled over and sat up. He felt like a man in a dream, yet the pain he suffered informed Mr. Jones that this was no dream, but a grim, incredible reality.

It was not alone the question, where was he, although that seemed pressing enough. But how had he gotten into the water at all? The last thing he remembered was a little, pleasant, white-finished room— a state room—ah, that was it. He was in his state room on board the liner. He was on board the Lusitania, and he was going to London to visit his cousin, the Hon. Percy Merridale. And he had—let's see, he had been going over the things in his steamer trunk with his man, Philip. And then—then he was going to bed. He must have gone to bed, and then-

He cudgeled his memory, but failed to beat out one single further recollection back of that dazed, strangling moment when he had found himself struggling with the waves.

Where was the liner? While in the water he could not recall having seen any lights, receding or otherwise. Stare earnestly as he might now across the sea, there were certainly no lights visible other than the stars, which storm-clouds now obscured at ever-increasing intervals.

Where was the Lusitania? And how had he come to part company with her so inexplicably? If the huge ship had melted away from about his slumbering form like a dream thing, instead of the vast solid steel hulk she was, she could not have vanished more thoroughly or mysteriously.

Only one explanation occurred to Mr. Jones, and even that was inadequate to explain the liner's total disappearance. When a boy he had been given to the habit of sleep-walking. He had usually slept locked in, in those days, but had thought the habit long since dead and gone. Nevertheless, he must have risen in a dream, gone on deck, and in some way fallen over the rail without being seen by any one.

What an extremely awkward predicament! Where could he be? What land lay near enough for him to have reached it undrowned? In view of the approximate position of the liner, so far as he knew it, Ireland seemed the only possible answer to that question. Had he been cast upon some portion of the Irish coast? Certainly the only thing for him to do was to get up and walk along this lonely, God and man forsaken beach until he came to some place where he could get dry clothes and cable his friends in London.

His clothes! He was fully dressed, and he examined the garments as well as he was able by starlight. They seemed wrong, some way. They were not his clothes, at all, but the clothes of a stranger. Had he, in his sleep, wandered into a neighboring stateroom and robbed some innocent stranger? He recalled that he had been talking to Philip about burglars and pistols—lightly it is true, but perhaps the suggestion of that conversation had led him into such an astounding exploit.

Mr. Jones searched this hypothetical other person's pockets, but all he brought to light were some wet, useless matches, a small penknife, an unmarked handkerchief, and a little loose change. There were no letters or anything by which the rightful owner could be identified.

By a mighty effort Jones forced the problem of the clothes out of his mind and fixed it upon the greater one of finding shelter and means of communication with London.

While he sat there the sky had completely cleared, and even by starlight he could make out that he was on a long, bare stretch of sand, which curved smoothly away on either side. From the inner edge of this strip a black wall of rock rose sharply, looming to the stars above Jones's head. This enormous cliff also curved away on either hand, following the line of the beach.

Selecting a quarter from the small coins he had found, Mr. Jones flipped it into the air. "Heads to the right, tails to the left," said he. The coin fell with the eagle uppermost and the castaway obediently started off in the direction indicated by Fate.

Walking was easy on the smooth, wet sand. The night air was so warm that even in his wet clothes Jones was not uncomfortably cold, and although the interminable breakers still roared in almost to his feet, the storm had evidently blown itself out. These rushing seas were only the aftermath.

Presently the beach dwindled away to nothing, and the cliff extended itself into the sea in a sort of long, sloping foot of jagged rocks. Mr. Jones managed to feel his way around this point, drenched again with spray, and wading through shallow pools of water. He tore his clothes and scraped his hands raw, but at last achieved the place where the beach began again.

"Halt!" commanded a stern, uncompromising voice.

Before him loomed the dark bulk of a figure which seemed to be pointing something at him. The figure came closer and the "something" developed into an unpleasant-looking rifle, along whose leveled barrel the starlight glimmered. Behind the figure, a hundred yards or so, Jones, saw a yellow gleam of lights, and not far out to sea, on the comparatively quiet waters of a little bay, some sort of vessel lay at anchor.

"Halt!" the man of the rifle again exclaimed in yet harsher tones.

"I have halted," replied Mr. Jones mildly. "May I ask—"

"None of your lip!" said the stranger ferociously. "Who are youse, and what do youse want around here?"

"Nothing—nothing at all. I was just walking along the beach—"

"Ho! Takin' y'r evenin' stroll up Fift' Avenoo, was youse? Well, just stroll along ahead of me now, and no more of your lip. I'll turn youse over to the captain, see? Now, march!"

Perforce Jones marched. He was unarmed, but even if he had carried the automatic pistol (and known how to use it) he could not see what would be gained by opposing this determined and ruffianly person. He stumbled along ahead of his captor, who occasionally hastened his footsteps by prodding him in the back most uncomfortably with his rifle-muzzle.

Luckily it was not far to the lights, where Jones presently discovered that three small tents were erected on the sand.

Another man came forward to meet them. He was a tall, well set-up figure. Even by the dim light of three ship's lanterns, set about in the sand, Jones could see that he was handsome, after a dark, foreign manner, and generally rather aristocratic in appearance. Neatly attired in white-ducks and of a fairly amiable expression, he seemed to Jones far preferable to his first acquaintance.

"What is this, Doherty?" inquired the gentleman in white.

"Youse c'n search me, y'r excellency," replied the man with the rifle. "I found it up there by the point, and I brung it into camp for youse fellers to cut up or keep, just as you please. I don't—"

"That will do, Doherty," broke in the other, a shade of annoyance in his even, cultivated voice. "You may return to your post And now," turning to the castaway, "who are you, sir, and how did you come here?" He spoke courteously and with the slightest trace of foreign accent in his otherwise faultless English.

Several other men had now gathered about them. They were roughlooking fellows, unshaven, and with dull, uneducated faces. Their costumes were not elaborate, consisting mostly of a shirt and a pair of more or less ragged trousers, the only exceptions being the man in white and a tall, powerful-looking brute of a fellow who was dressed in a blue serge uniform, like a ship's officer.

The moment had come for Mr. Jones to relate the tale of his strange misadventure and receive the aid and sympathy to which he knew himself entitled and which he fully expected to get, since rough clothes are by no means the natural insignia of unkind hearts.

"My name is Roland C. Jones," he began. "I am an American, and during the storm I was cast up on the beach—over beyond that point. By the way, is this the coast of Ireland?"

"Is this—what?" exclaimed the man in white with a look of intense astonishment.

"Oh, isn't it?" stammered Mr. Jones, rather taken aback by the stranger's amazement. "Well, you see I couldn't very well know what place it was. As I said, I was cast here by the storm, and of course I am very glad indeed to run across you fellows. That's a yacht you've got out there, isn't it? I thought by the look of her. I'm a yachtsman myself. My craft's the little Bandersnatch, New York Yacht Club."

These words should have been an open sesame to instant solicitude and hospitality, for to own a yacht is to belong to a sort of freemasonry, extending over the whole wide seas; but this stranger. only stared at Jones with increasing coldness and suspicion.

"Exactly," he commented briefly, his lips curling in a curious little smile. "And how did you come to be cast away? Has your yacht been wrecked? Did no one else come ashore? Where are your companions?"

In the teeth of this fusillade of questions Mr. Jones launched once more into his explanation.

"My yacht was not wrecked. I was not on my yacht. I was on board the Lusitania, and Heaven knows where she is now."

"Heaven probably does," interrupted the stranger, smiling coldly. "The Lusitania was torpedoed by a German submarine early this morning. We have but just received the information by wireless. If you were one of the victims you are indeed to be pitied. You have been forced to swim a very long way— several thousand miles, I think. Did you come around the Horn, or through the canal, my friend?"

Jones stared at him blankly. Was the man insane? Torpedoed—by Germans—thousands of miles! He clasped his head in his hands and groaned. It must be he himself who was mad. Then raising a very white face he spread out his arms in a gesture of despair.

"I'll have to admit that I don't know what you are talking about. I—I am afraid something has happened to my head—or I don't hear you correctly. No one could possibly torpedo the Lusitania—unless it were an anarchist, and I can't imagine what you mean by several thousand miles."

"That is sad. Yes, your brain must be affected, sir. You recollect that you are an American, and that is much, but I think you are mistaken about your name. Well, we will keep you with us. I do not really think it would be safe for you to stray about any longer alone in your pitiful condition. Captain Ivanovitch," he turned to the tall man in blue serge, "I will turn this young man over to you. You have heard him and will agree with me that it is wise to guard him carefully—against himself, of course. Do you understand?"

He still spoke in English, and it was in broken English that the captain replied. He spoke with a grin.

"Excellency, I und'stand. He have forgot his name. He have forgot even that there ees war. Have you suggest a name which he know perhaps better than that one he say?"

"Not yet. My friend, if I should address you as Richard Holloway, would it arouse no recollections in your mind?" The words were pleasant enough, but the voice was keen and cold as a winter wind.

Jones looked at the man in increased bewilderment. For the sake of peace and until he could escape from these madmen, had he better accept this now cognomen? Before he could make up his mind, "his excellency" turned aside with a short laugh. "Take good care of Mr. Holloway, Ivanovitch," he flung back over his shoulder. "It is just possible that we may arouse his memory and make him useful."

"Eester way," said the captain, with deceitful politeness, "eet is great pleasure to entertain you. So leetle we theenk Reechard Hol'way come to us so, free of weel. Weel you accept shelter from one of our leetle tents? Yes?"

Some inner instinct informed Mr. Jones that this Holloway personality was a dangerous one to assume. Playing himself off as another man did not appeal to him, anyway.

"I am not the person you seem to think I am," he said rather doggedly. "But I'd go anywhere to get something to eat. I'm nearly starved."

The captain grinned again, mockingly, hatefully. "At once, Meester Hol'way. We are all humbly servants. Dmitri—" Here he turned to one of the seamen who stood by staring stupidly and launched a command in some language which was unfamiliar to Jones, although, judging by the captain's own name and that of the man addressed, he assumed it to be Russian.

The sailor sprang to obey, and Captain Ivanovitch led Mr. Jones to one of the small tents. "Here," said he, "weel Meester Hol'way, permit to lodge himself. The tent, he is leetle, but you not mind that. Eet is more better than the ocean, no?"

"Humph! Perhaps," grunted Mr. Jones. He had taken an immediate dislike to the amiable captain. "By the way, you people seem to be very chary of introductions. Who is that gentleman I was just now speaking to? Your owner, I presume?"

"You not know? But of course. I forget you have jus' been sheepwreck. That ees his highness, Preence Sergius Petrofsky. The name also—it call nothing to your mind?"

"Nothing but Siberia and—er—Russian cigarettes. So, he's a connection of the royal family, is he? Now, tell me, what is all this fuss about, this man Holloway? There's no particle of use in calling me Holloway any longer, you know. I never even knew one of that name."

"So sad, Meester Hol'way. Perhaps you receive the blow upon the head—from wreckage, you und'stand? Eef you will show the place, we try to play the good part. We weel put upon eet the bandage."

"My head is all right, I tell you. My stomach is the only part of me that is in need of attention."

"Ver' good. Here come my man now weeth the good food. We shall not starve you, my friend. Also comes once more hees excellency."

The prince indeed came up at that moment. His features were set in a haughty frown, and he addressed himself immediately to Mr. Jones in a domineering tone.

"See here, Holloway, I have been considering this matter carefully, and can see no reason for your continuing the farce. How you came to fall into our hands is your own affair. But you must not rely upon the fact that your face is unfamiliar to us. There can be no question of your identity. You are the only man on the island—at least on the outside of it, for you yourself are theonly person who knows what is inside—who did not come here in the Monterey. Which places you beyond the shadow of a doubt as Richard Holloway. Now, answer me, yes or no. Will you tell me where lies the entrance to the caverns? If you help us we will make it well worth your while."

"What caverns?" queried Jones impatiently and with rising anger. These Russians were intolerable.

"Your feigned ignorance will not help you in the least, my friend," replied Petrofsky sternly. "I mean, of course, the caverns that lead beneath the cliffs. Out of all the caverns, the one which leads to that inner valley of yours. It was your story and yours alone which brought my brother across half a world to seek it.

"Come, sir, it is true that all of us here belong to the Brotherhood, and Paul has poisoned your mind against us. Also, by American eyes, I know that the great cause of nihilism is regarded askance.

"That is because you have experienced nothing of the evils which we plan to correct. But at least you know that I am a gentleman. If I give my word, I keep it. My brother has your trust."

"I am glad to hear it," murmured Jones wearily.

"What is that? I say that I, too, am a Petrofsky, and I swear to you that neither Paul nor those with him shall suffer the very least harm if you will help me. Nay, I will go further and promise that he shall receive his full share of the gains. The cause will not begrudge him that, although he has done his utmost to thwart our participation in this venture. But he and his little party can do nothing now. They have scarcely any provisions, hardly any arms or amunition. We could sweep down and annihilate them at this moment if I did not always remember that Paul is indeed my brother. Come, Mr. Holloway save him against himself and for the time at least cast in your lot with us. Will you give me your hand on it?"

Jones hesitated. To him this long rigmarole of nihilists and caverns failed to carry any meaning whatsoever.

"How can I convince you, Sir," he said at last, "that I know nothing whatever of these matters? That all I desire is to get away from this place and continue my quiet, respectable journey to London. And last and most emphatically that my name is certainly not Holloway, but Roland C. Jones, of New York City. You are making a serious mistake, Prince Petrofsky, and a most absurd one, if you will pardon me."

The Russian's eyes flashed angrily.

"Ho! You are yet stubborn? We will see if we cannot loosen your tongue a bit. Now, listen to me, and remember that I pledge my word as a Petrofsky that this promise will be kept. If you persist in your present attitude you will be taken on board that yacht and triced up to the signal-mast. Then you will be beate—they beat criminals in Russia. With the knout. Do you know what the knout means? I can see by your expression that you do. Well, make up your mind which it is to be. You may expect either our gratitude or—the other! You have until morning to decide. While making up your mind you may remain in that tent. Ivanovitch, set a guard over this man and see that he does not escape. Mr. Holloway, I give you a very good evening!"

Sergius Petrofsky turned his straight white back upon the dismayed American and stalked off down to the shore. There he got into a waiting dingey and was rowed out to the yacht.

Jones started, shivering slightly, as the captain touched his elbow and said in a soft voice, "You are foolish man, Meester Hol'way. But do not be so foolish as try leave us to-night. You und'stand?"

And Mr. Jones was left with his guard of two bearded sailors.

"Good Lord!" he muttered to himself. "What a crazy mess! Is knouting any worse than drowning, I wonder? I'll bet it is!"

CHAPTER II

Midnight found Mr. Jones sitting in his prison tent disconsolate.

There was a neat cot and blankets, but he had never felt less like sleeping in his life. He clung to his wakefulness and the few hours intervening between him and the morrow, like a sick man anticipating an extremely painful but inevitable operation. For something told him that Sergius Petrofsky was not the man to make empty threats.

Mr. Jones could see no way out of his predicament—unless he might anger the Russian into shooting instead of torturing him. The man certainly possessed a violent temper behind those haughty eyes of his.

While the captive was still revolving in his mind this desperate expedient, he suddenly felt something poke him sharply in the back. At the same instant some one said "Sh!" in a sharp, sibilant whisper.

The pain of the unexpected jab made Jones spring to his feet, crashing into the tent-pole and shaking the whole tent so violently that one of his guards appeared in the entrance. He thrust a large, hirsute countenance into the aperture and said something that sounded like the name of a Russian province.

"Get out, get out!" exclaimed Mr. Jones, gesturing violently to make his meaning clear. "It is nothing at all. Nothing. I bumped into the pole. Go away!"

The guard stared at him suspiciously for a moment longer, glanced about the little tent, which was dimly lighted by a lantern, and at last withdrew himself.

Once more the prisoner sat down, close to the canvas wall, and cautiously whispered, "It's all right. He has gone. Who are you and what do you want? What did you poke me like that for?"

There was a moment's silence, followed by a slight ripping sound. Through the canvas close by his shoulder Jones saw the point of a knife appear. It deftly cut two sides of a small triangle, then the flap so made was lifted and a face appeared. The face looked familiar. Then Mr. Jones recognized Doherty, the man who had captured him.

"Say, where are youse from?" The question was barely breathed in a voice which could not possibly have carried beyond the walls of the tent. Jones replied in the same bated tone:

"New York. Why?"

"That settles it, bo. Wait a jif."

The face was withdrawn, and the knife came into use once more. This time, however, it sawed out an aperture about three feet square near the bottom of the canvas wall. "Come on out, bo," whispered the rescuer.

Mr. Jones obeyed, moving as stealthily as he could, and having first made sure that the lantern would not cast the shadow of his escaping form upon the side of the tent. The situation required caution if ever a situation did.

Once outside he straightened himself, and felt a powerful hand grasp his arm. "This way, bo," came the whisper, and rescuer and rescued crept softly across the sands, behind the tents, and away, keeping close to the cliff. Glancing seaward, Jones saw the riding lights of the yacht, otherwise a dim, black bulk upon the quiet waters of the bay.

His guide led him away from the camp, not in the direction of the point where the two had first met, but onward along the beach. As soon as they were out of ear-shot of his Russian companions Doherty halted and said:

"I don't go no furder wid youse, see? G'wan on along until youse comes to a ravine. Go up there, and pretty soon youse comes to where dis other prince guy is, see? I don't know whether youse and this Holloway feller are the same guy or not. If you are, then youse don't need no more help from me. If youse ain't, then take a tip and hold your jawr about comin' straight from this camp, see? Now, beat it!"

"But see here!" exclaimed Jones, laying his hand on the other's shoulder to stay him. "Why have you helped me out this way? I'm everlastingly obliged to you, and—"

"Aw, ferget it!" snapped the other, shaking off the detaining hand roughly. "I ain't no friend of youse, neither, see? But no Russian dook ain't my boss when it comes to beatin' up another N'York feller with that knout thing. See? Now, will youse beat it, or d'youse want t'go back there and get what's comin' to youse?"

"I'll go. But, thank you, just the same. Say, can't you tell me something about all this business—"

But already Doherty had disappeared in the darkness, and with a slight sigh Roland C. Jones turned his face in the direction he had been instructed to follow. At any rate, the knouting was indefinitely postponed, and he could think of nothing much worse which could befall.

A short distance beyond the place where Doherty had left him the beach again ended in rocks. The man had spoken of a "ravine," so Mr. Jones again climbed and scrambled, coming at last to where the cliff seemed to be split in two parts. How far this split penetrated into the rocky wall, he had no means of knowing, for it was all as dark as a pocket.

He discovered by stumbling into it that a little rill of water flowed down the middle of the split and into the sea. His best chance of exploring the ravine was to walk up the bed of this stream, which was no more than ankle deep. The water, he found, had the bitter chill of a glacier stream, and his feet were soon numb with cold. He had been offered no opportunity to dry his clothing, and it was still very damp and uncomfortable. He hoped that the extreme warmth of the night might prevent him from getting pneumonia.

Mr. Jones was not accustomed to such privations and hardships, and he found them extremely annoying.

Having no means of making a light, he stumbled along in the darkness, alternately cursing himself for having fallen overboard and the Hon. Percy Merridale as the (however remote) cause of all his misfortunes.

At length, however, the watercourse made a sharp bend, and rounding it, he beheld, a short distance ahead of him, a reddish glow upon the rocks. Then a black figure appeared in silhouette against the glow. He was considering how he could best make his presence known, for this he correctly surmised to be the place of that mysterious other encampment, when a voice exclaimed, "Hands up, there, or I'll fire!"

"Twice in one night!" muttered Jones rebelliously.

"What's that? Stranger, you've strayed onto the wrong range. Come into the light, and don't make no false moves, or you'll sure get perforated."

The voice had now come close to his side, and Mr. Jones felt the hard muzzle of some sort of weapon pressing against his ribs.

"I assure you that I am not armed," he said.

"I'll assure myself in a minute," responded the unsympathetic voice. "March, now!"

And again Jones marched. The light which Jones had seen reflected upon the cliff was cast by a fire built between two huge boulders in such a manner as to obscure its radiance so far as was possible. Emerging into the full glare, the unfortunate halted again, obedient to the pressure on his arm.

About the fire, which they were probably maintaining for the sake of illumination, since they were cooking nothing, and the temperature of the night was so high, several figures were gathered. All save one of these persons were men, the exception being a slender young girl, who at that moment turned her face and stared straight into the eyes of Mr. Jones.

"By Jupiter!" he murmured. "What's a girl like that doing with this crowd?"

The young lady was attired in a somewhat dilapidated white yachting costume, which looked as if it had been soaked more than once and not pressed in a long time. But she was not of the type whose social standing or personal attraction would ever be judged by her clothes, however she might be dressed. Her crisply curling hair gleamed almost red in the firelight, though in daytime it would probably be no more than auburn. Her skin was of that clear, transparent whiteness which sometimes accompanies such hair; her features clean-cut and firm to a point which would have been almost masculine had they not been relieved by, a pair of blue eyes so pure, childish, and innocent that looking at them one could only be reminded of the eyes of a suddenly awakened baby.

For the rest, she was slight of figure, with small, tapering hands and feet, giving an impression of physical weakness which Mr. Jones later discovered to be deceptive.

He did not, of course, absorb all these details of appearance in that first brief meeting. At the moment he saw only that here was a beautiful, well-bred girl in the midst of surroundings entirely unsuitable—unless she happened to be a movie actress, which seemed improbable.

Of her companions, one was a tall, rather good-looking man with a sensitive mouth and slightly receding chin, also in yachting costume. Another was a rangy, lanky sort of fellow, attired in nothing more formal than a shirt and shabby trousers. The two remaining men were plainly of a lower class, probably seamen from their general appearance.

With a look of astonishment the girl glanced from Jones to his captor, who stood slightly behind him, and said:

"James, who is this person? How did he come here?"

Yes, she said it exactly as if she were standing in her own drawing-room, inquiring of the butler how some unknown vagabond had penetrated into her domain. Something humorous in the whole situation smote Jones abruptly, so that he laughed aloud, and she stared at him more haughtily than ever.

"I beg your pardon," said Mr. Jones, hastening to correct his involuntary rudeness, "I have had a rather trying evening, and—er—I did not expect to see a young lady in this place."

"And why not, pray? You are one of Prince Sergius' friends, are you not? Paul, this must be one of your brother's men, although I for one have never seen him before. Do you know him?"

She addressed the handsome man with the weak chin, and Jones knew this must be the brother of the Russian who had imprisoned him.

"No," he replied, rising lazily. "I have never seen the fellow before. Do you know him? Dick Holloway?"

"Not yet, but I've no objection. What is your name, anyway?"

So the man in the shirt and trousers was Holloway. Jones looked at him with considerable interest, since it was in his name that he had nearly suffered so much, and saw that he was a young man with a keen, rather strong face. Dressed differently, he might have been either a reporter or an automobile salesman—or a member of Jones's own club.

"My name is Roland C. Jones," stated the castaway, somewhat weary of reiterating that fact. "Some hours ago, early in the evening, I was cast up on the beach by the storm. I—think I had fallen overboard in my sleep. I was on my way to London. Then I—" He suddenly remembered Doherty's warning. He decided that he owed it to his benefactor to keep faith. "I came on up the beach and stumbled into this ravine and walked up it and—and here I am, you know."

This simple statement was met by dead silence for a moment. Then the Russian asked: "You were going to London, you say? That sounds a little peculiar. And you say you were wrecked, some hours ago? Where were you, pray, in the interval? Do you mean you have met no one since that time?"

"Yes," admitted Mr. Jones, realizing that his story lacked strength. "I met one man—or, rather, I saw a man; but as soon as he caught sight of me he made off. I chased him, but he was too quick. Then I wandered around a while, until I found my way here."

"H—m What ship were you on?"

Jones started to reply, "The Lusitania," but checked himself. He was actually afraid that these people, too, would insist on that nightmare tangle of German torpedoes and impossible distances. Then he would know that something had crone wrong in his brain. He did not want to know it just then. There was too much to attend to without that. "I was on my own yacht, the Bandersnatch. We were just cruising around, you know. We had thought of running over to the Azores." (Jones was not at all sure by this time where in the Atlantic he might be, but the Azores, as occupying a fairly central position, seemed safe.) "I must have walked in my sleep, for first thing I knew I was in the water, and the only wonder is that I was not drowned. I am a New Yorker, but we sailed from Savannah." He was rather proud of this touch of realism, but Holloway burst out laughing.

"First London, and now the Azores," the latter remarked in a tone of goodnatured amusement. "You seem to have put out on a remarkable voyage."

"For my part," interposed the young lady, who, despite her infantile eye, seemed of very determined and decisive character, "I don't believe a word of your story. If you were on a yacht, which I don't doubt, it was the Monterey, and she lies in the bay now. I believe you were on board at the same time we were, although we didn't see you. That about London and Savannah and the Azores is merely ridiculous. I can't imagine your object in making such absurd statements. Paul, this man has been sent here by your brother to spy upon us and find out the secret of the caverns."

Paul nodded his head, saying: "Holloway, do you not think that Miss Weston is right?"

"It's a one best bet she is, prince. All that gas about his yacht and the rest of it was probably planned to make us think he's a bit light in his upper story."

"What?"

"Bats in his belfry—nobody home—you know."

"Oh, you mean insane. But why should he wish us to think that?"

"So we won't take too much pains to keep our cards face down. If you'll take a tip from me, prince, you'll keep this angel-faced little castaway tied right to mama's apron-strings till time's called."

The prince laughed amiably, but the amiability was for Holloway, not Mr. Jones.

"Your expressions—your idioms—they are so very charming, Dick Holloway. But you are right. We cannot afford to be betrayed. James Haskins, you will kindly remain close to this gentleman's side. Take him with you and return to your post. And now, my friends, we have already sat too long talking. Let us sleep for the two hours that remain of night. Remember, we start at dawn."

CHAPTER III

As if stricken dumb, Mr. Jones obeyed the guiding hand of James Haskins, as it steered him back to the point whence he had first sighted the camp-fire. It seemed as though something even stronger than Fate were against him. Whatever he said was turned back upon him; whatever he did, it merely led him into fresh disaster. There was no use in fighting the tide. Henceforth he would keep still and permit events to shape themselves, unhelped or hindered by his efforts.

Perhaps, presently, he would wake up. Yes, this must be some unusually vivid nightmare which had him in its clutches.

"Squat right down on that rock, stranger, and make yourself at home." Of course, it was Haskins who broke in on his reverie. "If any more mavericks stray off your range up this way, I'll be right here to throw, tie, and brand 'em. Have a cigarette?"

"No—Yes, thank you, I believe I will."

For a few moments the two smoked without speaking. The night was silent, save for the low, distant murmur of the sea and the occasional squeak of a bat. Overhead the great, brilliant stars, which hung so strangely low and near, seemed to wink at Jones, as if they were sharers in some huge joke of whose nature he was not yet informed, but of which he was unquestionably the butt.

"Strange," he reflected. "I can't remember ever having smoked in a dream before. I can taste the tobacco, too. And my hands hurt like the dickens, where I scraped 'em on the rocks. I wonder if I ever will wake up. That girl is a winner for looks, all right; but, oh, mama, I don't like her disposition one little bit! Seems to have it in for me, all right. I wonder—"

"Pleasant dreams!" It was James Haskins again. "Say, did you really get washed ashore like you told the bunch?"

"I certainly did," said Jones with convincing vigor and promptitude. "Look here; if I should tell you the whole story about what has happened since I reached this place, would you believe me?"

"Fire away!" the other replied noncommittally.

Jones obeyed, and his jailer listened patiently and in silence to the full tale of his misadventures. Barring the fact that it was a liner and not his own yacht from which he had fallen, he adhered closely to facts; for, in the light of his reception, it seemed it was only for his own good that Doherty had warned him not to speak of the other camp. And in this opinion his listener presently confirmed him.

"So this man Doherty told you not to tell you'd been in his camp, did he?" was Haskins's comment at the end of the recital. "Well, he, was dead right, friend castaway. Prince Paul has got just the same love for Prince Sergius that a grizzly has for a rattlesnake.

"But me, I think you're straight. For one thing, you haven't got the map of a bunco-steerer; and for another, I think you are because size thinks you ain't. Do you get me? I never saw anything in skirts yet that you couldn't copper her guess and be on the right trail. Only your swim seems to have twisted your geography some. It isn't the Azores you mean—it's the Philippines, or Hawaii. Now, if you and me should swap yarns, will you give me away to my outfit, or will you keep it under your hair?"

"Prince Sergius' knout wouldn't extract it from me," sighed Mr. Jones, with the happy sense that here again, where least expected, he had found a friend.

"Well, to commence with, me, I'm riding a long way off my own range, which is Colorado, by rights, though I was born in Arizona. Arizona Jim, that's me. Well, this prince fellow come along when I was on my uppers in Frisco, having gone up against a few large doses of redeye and an outfit of card-sharks some simultaneous. But, say, you fellows started from Savannah, you said. Did you get into the Pacific through the canal?"

The Pacific? Jones's brain reeled again, but he managed to keep his voice steady and reply: "Yes, of course we went through the canal."

"I asked because I know a fellow that runs a cafe in Colon. Did you stop there?"

"I didn't go ashore there. But how did you meet the prince?"

"Oh, yes. Well, as I was saying, he met up with me, and he offers me a job. Says he's goin' on a big trip and wants a guy with a good gun-eye. That's me, all right; so I joins the outfit immediate. Then's when I meet this brother of his, they bein' on good terms then, just like an owl and a prairie-dog.

"So brother Sergius, it seems, he's gone right ahead and chartered a yacht without waiting for brother Paul to approve the deal. This annoys us some, but not half so much as when we get away out on the broad, be-yutiful, lonesome Pacific Ocean and finds that the captain and the crew are all 'brothers' of his, too. Yes, little Annie, Sergius is in with the anarchists, saddle, bridle, and spurs, and the great and noble cause has got to get its share in the profits, even if brother Sergius has to knife brother Paul to do it. Oh, yes, it was some rotten deal, take it from me."

"But where does this Miss ... Miss—"

"Weston come in? Not yet but soon. We picks Miss Weston up out of an open boat, along with a couple of half-dead sailors. She's a Boston young lady that's been taking lessons in nursing. She aims to join the Red Cross, but she's some foxy, so she comes clear across to Frisco and takes a boat for Japan, figurin' to get into the festivities by the back gate, so to speak. No German torpedoes in hers."

(Jones gave a mental groan. Again!)

"And right then, was when the lid blew off the kettle for keeps. I never did see two brothers take a shine to the same girl quite so simultaneous and sudden. Gee, they ought to have been twins, their tastes are so similar. Was she going to be Princess Sergius or Princess Paul? I suggests to Paul, casual-like, that they cut her in two and divide her up, it being my idea that there ain't any female woman born that's any real good in a round-up like this one. But he didn't seem to take to it.

"So brother Paul, he reveals to her the perfidy of brother Sergius, and right away that swings her. No nihilanarchists for hers. In which she shows more sense than I'd expected.

"Right about then we sights this here Joker Island. Some name, Joker; but she's some Island, too, believe me. There being considerable hard feeling, what with one thing and another, me and Prince Paul and this Weston girl and her two sailors, we thinks it wise and becoming to withdraw ourselves from evil associations, and we drops off the yacht the first dark night. Then Prince Paul he says there's a guy on the island expecting him, which is the first I heard of Holloway. As near as I can make out, this is Holloway's island, by right of being wrecked here and finding out some darn thing about the inside of it. These cliffs go all the way around, you know, but there's a cave runs under 'em, and Mr. Holloway, he's the only one that knows where it is."

"I shouldn't think it would be very difficult to find a cave in a wall of rock like this, if one hunted for it," suggested Jones, deeply interested in the narrative.

"Oh, no, it's dead easy—like three guesses at which is the right hole in a colander. There's about fifteen hundred other caves, and they all run back under the cliffs, and there's only one that goes clear through. And if you get lost in a blind lead—good night!"

"But what is there inside, anyway?"

"Me not being Prince Paul's confidential secretary, I don't know, nor I don't know how Sergius thinks he's going to get there without dear brother Paul and friend Holloway. But it's plain he knows something about Holloway, or he wouldn't have made that nice, kind offer to persuade you when he thought you was Holloway. One thing, it's clear he don't know him by sight. The way I figure it is that when Holloway was wrecked here, after he comes out of the inside again, he was taken off by some ship, and then he hikes right after Prince Paul, who, it seems, is his dear old college chum. It must be some secret, all right; for Paul, he gets leave immediate from his regiment by the Czar's special permit.

"But brother Sergius, who's some unpopular at home, he don't need no permit, because he's in America already. I don't think Paul was lookin' to run across him; but when he does, he takes him in on the deal for the sake of them old days back on the farm. Well, while Paul is rustling this outfit together, friend Richard gets himself put on the island alone again, with provisions, and stays right on the claim to wait for Paul. Paul comes along with a brother and a aggregation of nihilanarchists and a Boston schoolmarm girl, and now the only way out is in."

"What?"

"Just like I says—in. We're going through the caves at daybreak. Holloway says even he might get the wrong one at night."

"Good Lord!" murmured Mr. Jones softly. From boyhood he had suffered from a dread of dark, shut-in places, running parallel, perhaps, with his habit of sleep-walking. Even now be never slept without a light in his room, and he would not have explored the Mammoth Caves with a guard of fifty guides for all the money in the world. "Are you—are they going to take me along?"

"What's the matter? Don't you want to sit in? Take it from me, you're better off with Paul than you would be with Sergius, and you've only got Paul and Sergius to choose between."

"What sort of lights are you going to use?" queried Mr. Jones anxiously.

"Oh, we have some electric torches. Stranger, I've talked myself into the finest thirst outside of Arizona. But it's wasted—absolutely wasted. Ain't that a sad thought? By gracious, I'd almost go over and take up with this naughty Sergius party, if I thought he had anything stronger than water to give me. But, alas! The Monterey is like Russia—she's gone prohibition. Don't you notice a different feeling in the air? What time's it getting to be?" He glanced at his watch.

"'What time were you intending to start?" inquired Jones.

"Half an hour. It's three now. Here comes Holloway."

CHAPTER IV

"Did you catch any more bugs, Jim?" called Richard Holloway cheerfully as he approached. "No? Too bad. Hoped we could start a collection. Say, Mr.—er, what did you say your name was? Something unusual, wasn't it?"

"Jones," replied the castaway rather stiffly. He was a trifle tired of the disdainful attitude which every one except the cowboy had so far assumed toward him. "Roland C. Jones."

"Mr. Roland C. Jones, I salute you." Holloway bowed very low and straightened with a laugh. "Did you leave any last will and testament with his serene and nihilistic highness when he sent you over here? Because, you know, it's just possible that something might happen to you inside. You've no idea how wonderfully exciting 'inside' is, Mr. Jones. Don't let me alarm you, though."

Jones laughed almost hysterically. "It can't be much more exciting than—than everything else," he said. "And as for getting killed, I'm beginning to have a suspicion that that's the best thing which could happen to me."

He was thinking of his own mental condition, but Holloway understood him differently.

"So bad as that?" he asked with mock commiseration. "No home? No friends? Somebody cooked your chestnuts for you? Never mind, sweet child. We'll buy you some more—if we ever get off Joker Island. Coming, Prince?" he called back, as a voice hailed him from the little camp. "Come on, Jimmy; and you, too, Rolly! You don't mind if I call you Rolly? I feel in my heart that we're going to be friends, Rolly, and what's a name between pals?"

"I don't care what you call me," replied Mr. Jones, smiling in spite of himself. After all, there was something very likeable about this impertinent, goodnatured fellow. He felt that he could get along very nicely if he had nobody but the cowboy and Richard Holloway to deal with.

They found the rest of the party eating a very informal breakfast, consisting of hardtack, a few rashers of bacon, and some really excellent coffee. Jones received his share thankfully. He could not remember a time when he had been so hungry, or hungry so often, as in the few hours since he had come to Joker Island.

Then the fire was extinguished; what provisions were left and some simple impedimenta were divided equally among the men, and the expedition started with only Miss Weston unburdened. She tripped lightly along beside her Russian admirer, apparently as merry and light-hearted as if they were bound on a picnic.

Dawn had come upon them with extraordinary suddenness as they ate, it seemed to Mr. Jones. There had been a few moments of ghostly twilight. Then the sun leaped into the sky, like a tiger springing from its lair, and flung at them his first rays with an ardor which promised insufferable heat later on.

Now that it was light, Jones perceived that the ravine, or split in the cliff wall, ended abruptly just beyond the camp. There the precipice towered as forbidding and unscalable as it hung above the outer beach. The little stream sprang from a mere crevice in the otherwise solid wall. There were certainly no caverns in that direction, and he was not surprised when Holloway, in his capacity of guide, led the way back down the ravine toward the sea; but he did wonder how they could emerge upon the beach without being seen by the nihilists.

They had followed the watercourse only a short distance, however, when Holloway turned aside and led them into a yet narrower crack in the rocks which branched off from the main ravine. The going became more and more difficult, and Paul Petrofsky was obliged to almost carry the girl over some places, while the rest of the party scrambled and sweated and swore sotto voce.

At last the crack widened; they caught a glimpse of blue beyond, and in another moment they came out upon a part of the beach which was cut off by a jutting promontory of rock from the small bay where the Monterey lay anchored. Jones thought that a bird's-eye view of that island must show the cliff to be fairly scalloped with little bays and promontories.

And here the black rock was honeycombed with dark holes, bored out either by the sea or by volcanic agency; some of them no more than a foot or so across, a few large enough so that a motor-truck could have been safely driven in.

"This is only the beginning of 'em," declared Holloway, addressing Petrofsky, but in loud enough tones to be heard by all. "Half way 'round the island the rock is fairly-perforated. Some place for a tribe of cave men, no?"

Then, suddenly assuming the manner of a tourist guide: "Just step this way, lady and gentlemen. Here you may behold the finest—oldest—most dog-gonedest aggregation of black holes—"

His voice died away and became indistinguishable, for he had dropped to hands and knees and crawled into one of the smaller caverns.

Petrofsky, pausing only to draw an electric torch from his pocket, immediately followed, and close upon his heels crept Miss Margaret Weston. To Jones's amazement, the girl was laughing just before she disappeared. He could not have laughed himself to win a medal. However, Jim Haskins and the two sailors were looking at him expectantly.

There was nothing else for it, so he, too, dropped to his knees and crawled into the hole, pushing ahead of him the small bundle which had been assigned him to carry. He wondered bitterly if they were to crawl all the way through the cliff.

Ahead of him he could see a moving black mass against a dim glow of light, which he knew to be the intrepid Miss Weston, of Boston, Massachusetts. Jones had no light himself, and was too far behind the leaders to get any benefit from theirs. The rock was wet and a trifle slimy. He thought of snakes, but remembered gratefully that if there were any they would have a good chance to bite three people before they got to him.

Behind, he could hear a grunting and scraping, and knew the other three were following.

Then the glow ahead abruptly disappeared, and there was a scrambling, thumping sound. Had Holloway and the Russian fallen into some abyss? He halted, but immediately after heard a voice calling, "Come ahead! It's all right! Oh, what a perfectly lovely, splendid place!"

It was the voice of Margaret Weston, and a moment later Mr. Jones scrambled out of the narrow hole into an enormous, scintillating cavern. The lights of two electric torches were reflected dazzlingly from a million fiery points.

"What perfectly gorgeous stalactites!" exclaimed the girl rapturously. "Oh, Mr. Holloway, I'm so glad you found this place! It's worth anything just to have seen it. Why, if it were not so hard to reach, this would be one of the show places of the world, would it not?"

"It would," admitted the flattered Mr. Holloway. "But I only wish I could let some sunlight into the hole for you. I've taken some pieces of this stuff out, and in daylight they are all colors of the rainbow. Look like stuff out of a jeweller's window. The colors don't show up in this light."

"Thank you, but it's quite beautiful enough as it is."

Even Jones had to admit to himself that Miss Weston was, in a measure, right. Above their heads was a black void. The roof was too high and probably too dark in color for their lights to show it, but all about them, depending almost to the floor, hung a thousand icicle-points, which reflected the electric rays as if they had been encrusted with diamonds. From the floor, also, rose points and mounds of brilliant crystals. This lower forest of stalagmites seemed to extend itself indefinitely, certainly beyond range of the torches.

"Dick Holloway," said the prince, "this is fairyland to which you have brought us. The air, too, which I had thought would be almost poisonous, it is fresh. It smells of the sea. There must be many more openings into this place than that by which we entered."

"There probably are," agreed Holloway, "but I'd hate to hunt for them. I was lost in these caves once—that was the way I happened to locate the way through—but I'd hate to risk it twice."

"But tell me," continued the prince, gazing upward curiously, "is there no danger from the falling of some of these huge masses from the roof?"

"Sure thing there is. But—Jimmy, there goes a beauty right this minute!"

There was an ominous crackling sound, the mild forerunner of a thunderous, deafening crash. The air was filled with a cloud of choking white dust, through which the torches gleamed faintly as through a fog. The noise was followed by a series of lesser crashes. Then came again the calm, unagitated voice of Holloway.

"Did that hit anybody? If it did, farewell to the dear departed. Is every one here?"

One by one the little party answered with their names, Jones last, and in a voice which he rendered steady with some effort. He had always known that caverns would be just like this. For a moment he had been deceived by the treacherous beauty of this one, but no more. Surely they would turn back now. Nobody could expect to pass through this place where at any moment a thousand pounds of glittering stalactite was liable to drop on him-

It was the voice of Miss Weston which answered his unspoken thought.

"Well, there is no need of our standing here, is there? How in the world can you find your way, Mr. Holloway?"

"Been here before," replied that gentleman cheerfully. "Know it like the streets of my hometown. Come along."

By this time the white dust had somewhat settled, and Jones could see his companions clearly. They were starting off single file between the innumerable stalagmites, apparently careless of disaster. On an impulse he crouched down behind a white mound.

Jim Haskins passed within hand's reach, but did not see him in the shadow. The two sailors were a little behind, and on a sudden thought Jones cautiously pushed his bundle of miscellaneous camp articles out from behind his mound.

An instant later one of the sailors stumbled over it, and as Jones had craftily foreseen, imagined that it had been dropped by one of the men ahead. Grumbling, the man picked it up and added it to his own load, and with no thought for a possible escaping prisoner, passed on.

In fact, nobody gave Mr. Jones a thought. He was alone, neglected and forsaken, and the fact gave him supreme relief. He had looked carefully, while there was still sufficient light, and a seen a black hole yawning, the hole by which they had entered this place of terror. Having honestly restored to his captors the goods with which he had been entrusted, Mr. Jones felt no scruples about deserting them.

Just before the last gleam of light from the electric torches faded and disappeared, Mr. Jones plunged back into the small tunnel and began rapidly wriggling his way toward open air and the blessed light of day.

Somehow or other the passage seemed much longer than when he had come that way at the heels of the Boston girl. Jones crawled and crawled, until his knees and elbows were sore, but still he could see no gleam of light ahead. It seemed to him that he had been crawling for hours. What could be the matter?

Suddenly the horrifying explanation dawned upon him. This was not the tunnel by which they had entered, but another of the labyrinthine system of caves to which Holloway had referred!

Mr. Jones stopped crawling and tried to turn himself about. There was not room enough, however, and he only hurt himself still more upon the slimy rock. There was no use in trying to wriggle backward, for he knew that he would become exhausted before he could ever regain the cave of stalactites by such a laborious process. Besides, he reflected, even if be did get back there he would be no better off. Surrounded by impenetrable midnight darkness, how could he hope to rediscover the passage he had been unable to identify while there was light?

With a sinking heart he contemplated the many hours of mental and physical suffering which lay before him if he should fail to extricate himself. He must go on. What a fool he had been to desert the party of adventurers! After all, they were kindly, honest folk and it would have been far better to have died suddenly by the fall of a stalactite, or in some merciful abyss, than here alone in the darkness of the damned.

He must get out! And when "must" drives, a man will do a great deal more than appears possible. Roland C. Jones did. He crawled literally for hours, turning, winding with the tunnel, like an unhappy and desolate angle-worm in the black bosom of Earth.

Once, exhausted, he let himself subside, and despite all the terrors of darkness went to sleep. He had not slept for v. long time, and when he awoke, though he ached in every limb, he felt refreshed and took new courage to crawl on.

Crawling is a slow process—at least, for a human being—but if a man crawl far enough, and encounters no obstruction, he is bound to get somewhere sometime, and that is what happened to Mr. Jones. He had long since given up all hope, and become a mere, dogged crawling-machine, when it happened. It was a tremendous thing and an experience which in all his after-life he never forgot. He saw the rock beneath him!

Then he raised his head, hopefully, prayerfully, and there, far ahead, beamed a glorious star of light!

Then did Mr. Jones perform prodigies of crawling. As if he had just started, he wriggled and scrambled along, and at last actually emerged from the black womb of death into the adorable, intolerable brilliance of day. Also into the very arms of Doherty, his former rescuer!

Behind Doherty stood Captain Ivanovitch, and beside him was Sergius Petrofsky. Mr. Jones had crawled windingly through the rock, all the way from behind the promontory, around the end of the ravine, and back to the little bay whereon the Monterey still lay at anchor.

He had expected anything—but not this. In the eternity which had elapsed since entering that black rat-hole he had forgotten that such a person as Sergius Petrofsky existed. His clothing was ripped to slimy rags. In a dozen places his body and limbs were scraped raw, he was faint and sick for lack of food and drink—and before him stood the man who had promised to torture him that day. The villainies of Fate were too prodigious.

Mr. Jones slipped suddenly from the sustaining grip of Doherty, and dropped in a wretched heap upon the sand.

CHAPTER V

When sense at last returned to the castaway, he opened his eyes and stared blankly about for a moment. He had dreamed that he was in his own bedroom in his own New York bachelor apartment, and these walls of brown canvas, that strange face bent above his, seemed incredible, far more visionary than the dream itself. Then the whiff of an agreeable odor reached his nostrils. Food! Mr. Jones sat up, and reached out his hands in one single motion. Doherty placed the bowl which he carried with them.

"I've brought youse your scoffin's," he said. "Gee! Youse was a sight when youse fell out of diat hole. His nibs is waitin' to see youse."

"Let him wait," commanded Jones in a determined voice. "Keep him out, can't you, till I finish this? This is the first thing I've had to eat for—for week's judging by the way my appetite feels."

Doherty laughed and seated himself on the side of the cot. "I'll tell him youse was pounding your ear so hard I couldn't wake youse up."

"Thanks, old man." There was an interval of silence, then Jones handed back the polished bowl with a great sigh, swung his legs to the floor and sat up. "Where are my clothes?" he asked.

"Your clothes? Gee, youse ain't got no clothes. There was a couple of old rags hangin' to youse, but if dat Anthony Comstock guy ever seen youse he'd t'row a fit, sure. Them things youse has on now belongs to the captain."

"But what am I to do? I can't walk around in these pajamas."

Doherty grinned. He seemed in an uncommonly good humor.

"Dat's all right. His nibs has came across wit' dese here glad rags. Climb, into 'em and look sharp, or I'll get the hide tore off me for keepin' him waitin'. There's a basin over there if youse wants to wash some more, but gee! They sure had to give you one bath before they could put youse to bed even."

"Well, I guess a little more water won't hurt me."

Jones also found a safety razor and a mug of luke-warm water beside the basin, and was glad enough to shave, although his beard was by this time a very stiff one to get rid of.

Then he dressed in the "glad rags" indicated by Mr. Doherty, which he found consisted of a suit of thin silk underwear, breeches and tunic coat of khaki, socks, puttees, and a pair of heavy, but wellmade shoes. In fact, as good an outfit for a tramping or hunting expedition as Jones could have bought anywhere in New York.

Very gratefully he donned the garments, which to his joy fitted him quite passably. The shoes were a little loose, but that was much more satisfactory than if they had been too tight.

He thought, as he dressed, that if they intended to abuse him—they had made a peculiar beginning. Sleep and food had done a great deal to bring him back to a normal outlook on life. His limbs still ached, but that was hardly strange in view of the strenuous character of recent experiences. Mr. Jones presently announced his readiness to go to or receive the waiting Sergius.

"Youse can wait here. I'll get him," said Doherty, who all the time preserved the same astonishing amiability. He did not even question Mr. Jones in regard to how he had come to return there, and not only return, but return in such a singular manner and condition. Some species of relief or joy fairly radiated from the man's every glance and word.

Mr. Jones did not have to wait long after Doherty's departure. He had gone to the entrance and stood looking out. The sun beat down from almost directly overhead, and he correctly surmised that this was the day following that on which he had emerged from the cave. He must have slept the clock fairly around.

Some distance up the beach a number of men were gathered about a large object which was partly obscured by an intervening tent, so that he could not quite make out its nature. In a moment he saw Sergius Petrofsky coming toward him alone.

"My friend," said the nihilist, glancing him up and down with a smile, "you have a much improved appearance."

"Thanks to you, Prince Sergius," asserted Jones, wondering yet more at the apparent friendliness of every one.

"You are entirely welcome, Mr. Holloway. But come inside, please. We must talk together."

They seated themselves, Jones on the cot, Sergius on the campchair.

"And now, Mr. Holloway, perhaps you will explain what has become of my brother and—and the young lady, Miss Weston."

So that was it. They had discovered that the other party had vanished into thin air and looked to him to recover the trail. Jones determined in his own honest mind that he would never discover to them the location of those caves. Besides, they might try to make him enter them again! But he could not feel that any loyalty to a party which had, after all, treated him only as a spy and a liar, demanded further sacrifice than this.

"In the first place, Prince Sergius, I am not Richard Holloway. When you found me I had never seen or heard of such a person, but since that time I have met the man himself."

Without reserve, save as regarded any implication of Doherty, Jones proceeded to tell his story, to which the Russian listened with an impassive face. At the end, however, he rose and extended his hand to his involuntary guest.

"I was mistaken, Mr. Jones, and I have to ask your forgiveness. We must have seemed to you not only inhospitable, but boorish in the last degree to so threaten you who deserved only our help and kindness. But your story of the Lusitania you yourself will admit was—well, let us speak no more of that. Perhaps some day you will entrust me with your full confidence. Now, however, you are in a position to extend to me a very great service.

"No—" he raised a protesting hand as Jones started to speak, "I do not longer ask that you reveal the cavern entrance. Your own experience shows what is the most likely fate of those attempting it without good guidance. We have done all in our power to make you forget our past unjust treatment, even while we still deemed you Richard Holloway. May I expect your favor in return?"

"Why, of course," replied Jones in some surprise. "But I don't exactly see what I could do—"

"You will see," said the prince, with a rather peculiar smile. "Will you be pleased to follow me?"

Together they left the tent and walked across the sands toward the object of which Jones had earlier caught a glimpse. Now he saw what it was. It was an aeroplane. The nihilist was again speaking:

"I had planned to take with me the man, Doherty, but he is an ignorant fellow, entirely unsuited to such an undertaking. Also, he was afraid to go. None other of the men are suitable. Ivanovitch, he must remain to look after our crew. My mechanic is ill on board the Monterey. The others are too stupid. They are fellow Russians and brothers in the cause, but you see I speak frankly. You, on the other hand, are young, intelligent, and—"

"You want me to go up in that thing with you?" gasped Mr. Jones.

"Of course. I am a good airman, You need feel no alarm, for in the air you will be in no danger. It is when we descend to what is within that I desire with me a reliable companion. Are we to be comrades?"

"You give me a choice?"

"But yes. Unless you come willingly, I would better make my flight alone."

"All right. I'll go."

Yes, it was really Roland Chesterton Jones, the coward of the caverns, who said these words! As a matter of fact, Jones was not a coward at all, but a victim of subconscious terror of the dark. Given a fair chance and the open air, he had always felt perfectly willing to face danger, although his life before coming to Joker Island had not been an adventurous one and he was by choice a young man of quiet life and manners.

The prince gave him an approving nod.

"I am not a bad reader of features. We will' meet everything like comrades, eh? And you will not be tempted, if we should come upon them, to return to my brother and his people?"

"I will not," said Jones firmly. He had nothing against any of them, but he possessed a natural predilection toward any one who treated him courteously, nihilist or not.

Moreover, there was something about Sergius Petrofsky which had attracted him from the first, in spite of his brutal threat that first night. Fanatical, cruel even, when thwarted, there was yet about him that invisible aura which we term personality, for lack of a better name. If he had been an actor he would undoubtedly have been an idol of the matinee girls. Jones wondered, when he thought of it, that Miss Weston had turned from him to his less attractive brother.

They had now reached the group of sailors gathered about the monoplane. Captain Ivanovitch was nowhere in sight, and they were lounging about in the sand, but all sprang to their feet at sight of Sergius. He said something sharply to them in Russian and all save two went off toward the tents. Then he turned again to his guest.

"I have been obliged to do almost all the work of assembling the plane with my own hands, because of this unfortunate illness of Thoreau, my mechanic. Are you in the least familiar with this sort of engine? It would be too much to hope that you know anything of the science of flight."

Mr. Jones hastened to disclaim any knowledge on either subject. He had always left even the mysteries of his own motor-cars, and his big power-boat, the Bandersnatch, to the expert attentions of their respective chauffeurs and captain. The most he knew about gasoline was that it sometimes exploded, and was used to drive automobiles, powerboats, and aeroplanes. Of the dark secrets of spark, ignition, carburetor, and so forth he was as innocent as a child.

"Then it is of no use for me to try to instruct you in the brief space which lies between us and departure. Your part will be to sit quiet in that seat which you see behind the pilot's place, and if we come to any grief I will endeavor to play the part of driver and mechanic also. We are taking with us no provisions, save a slight luncheon in that hamper, but these rifles may prove convenient. It is my purpose to make, as it were, a reconnaissance, and we may not even descend into the inner valley or crater until a later flight."

At this moment Captain Ivanovitch came up, accompanied by Doherty. The captain entered into conversation with Sergius in Russian, and as Mr. Jones waited for the next move, Doherty said in a low voice, "Gee, ain't I glad youse showed up? I ain't got no use for them flyin' things. If ever I gets to be a angel I suppose I'll have to flutter me wings—but till I gets 'em I sticks right to the ground floor."

"You may be right," Jones admitted.

"I thought we'd butt into the valley by the subway after all when I seen youse come out. But, gee, this lets little Willie out complete. Youse is welcome to the job."

"Mr. Jones," interrupted Sergius, "will you put these things on? It is not so warm up above there, you know."

He was holding out a heavy coat and a sort of hood, which Jones donned, while the nihilist put on a similar outfit. To the hood was attached a pair of large goggles which could be pulled down over the eyes. It was not a regular aviator's costume, but near enough for the short flight contemplated.

Then the two strangely assorted companions climbed to their places. Needless to say, it was the first time Mr. Jones had ever been in an aeroplane. He had attended meets, watched the daring evolutions of the dragon-flylike things against the sky, and had one or two opportunities to go up himself, but he had never experienced any desire to rise higher above solid earth than the top floor of a skyscraper.

Yet now he found himself strangely cool and unperturbed. Sergius Petrofsky inspired him with a great deal of confidence in his ability as a man of action.

Now Ivanovitch and a seaman had grasped the monoplane, one on each side at the rear, and were standing with feet braced as if expecting some great strain upon their muscles. Sergius did something with a lever and the engine burst forth into a roar which startled Mr. Jones extremely. He had forgotten what a racket the things make.

Then he felt a slight jerk and the plane was rolling swiftly along the sand. He was thrown back in his seat, as the machine tilted upward, and a moment later shut his eyes; for he had seen the beach dropping away from under them, and it seemed as if a violent wind had suddenly arisen. Remembering the goggles he reached up and pulled them down over his eyes before opening them again.

Glancing downward he saw the sea, rocking and swaying beneath them, had a moment of nausea, and realized that it was the plane which was rocking. They were up, they were actually flying through the air. The wind of their flight was beating upon his fate. The experience was different from anything which he had ever imagined, arid yet it was strangely exhilarating too. For the first time since he had found himself adrift in the sea, he was glad that he had fallen off the liner.

No matter what might befall, nothing could ever rob him of the memory of this moment when he learned the real meaning of man's victory over the air.

Sergius turned slightly and shouted something over his shoulder, but the roar of engine and propeller drowned his voice. Jones shook his head and shouted back something equally indistinguishable. He had meant to say "Grand! Glorious! Splendid!" but the wind seemed to hurl the words back down his throat.

He looked down again and saw to his amazement how high they had already climbed. The island lay beneath them, with that maplike appearance which one notices in bird's-eye views. The black cliff which had appeared so awesome and forbidding was now no more than a huge, irregular oval line of black. And this line surrounded—what? A sea of green, it seemed, probably the tops of trees, although the foliage was indistinguishable from that height. Moreover it all appeared to be swinging in vast circles, for they were ascending in a steep spiral.

Jones began to wonder how high they were to mount. He had imagined, in the brief time given him for thought, that they would simply rise above the cliff and immediately descend upon the other side.

Then, abruptly, the steady roar of the engine slackened and died. The nose of the plane dipped earthward and they were sliding down the air, swiftly, but so smoothly that the sensation was one of pure delight. The circles of their descent were so wide that, as they came nearer, Jones had plenty of time to study the strange valley which lay shut off from and unsuspected of the outer world.

That the island had been one huge volcanic crater at one time in its history, there could be no doubt. Now, however, there was nothing to suggest a volcano save the wall itself, and within was a wide expanse of the greenest verdure. The great oval was about ten or twelve miles long. Its floor was of a slightly undulating, parklike appearance, the upper, darker green being broken here and there by lighter patches which. Jones presumed to be little lawns and open glades in the forest.

The engine roared out again, but this time Sergius did not ascend. He turned so sharply that the plane "banked" at what seemed to his passenger an alarming angle, and shot straight across the valley. Then he once more cut out the engine and shot downward swiftly and steeply.

Suddenly Jones perceived what they were aiming at, a broad, smooth space of green, about a quarter of a mile in length, which the prince in his circlings had picked out for a landing place. An instant later dark masses shot upward on both sides, the pilot deftly straightened out the plane, and with a stiff jolt they had struck the earth.

The lawn, which had looked so smooth and even from above, proved to be an expanse of villainous hummocks over which they bounded and sprang for fifty yards or so, and at last came to a creaking, swaying halt.

CHAPTER VI

"That, my friend," cried Sergius, turning a beaming face, "that was a good landing, no? Coming down in such unknown country something is always liable to break, but we have better fortune."

"What funny-looking trees!" exclaimed Mr. Jones, paying no heed to the Russian's self-congratulations. "Why, they look like—like cabbages! And what a horrible smell!"

The word "horrible" was none too strong to describe the intolerable odor which permeated the air. Descending as they had done from the clear, clean, fresh upper atmosphere, it seemed at first almost impossible to breathe at all. It was a sort of concentrated, well-nigh visible stench, suggesting nothing less than decayed slaughter-houses or open graveyards. Even the prince lost his smile after the first moment of delight over his successful landing.

The "trees" to which Mr. Jones had referred, were indeed not trees at all, but some sort of vegetable growth entirely unfamiliar to either of the men. If they had really been the cabbages they resembled, they would have made the everlasting fortune of the market-gardener who grew them, for the smallest was as large as a fair-sized hen-house, and some of the larger ones must have measured at least a hundred feet from root to crest, with a diameter at least one fourth as great. They were a dark purple in color, shading upward into a sickly green. None of them grew very close together, and the spaces between were filled with an astonishing variety of mushroomlike things, whose vivid coloring, red, yellow, violet, and orange, jarred upon the eye in a disharmony of which nature is very seldom guilty.

Like a giant's vegetable garden, these monstrous growths entirely surrounded the glade where they had alighted. But even though they towered so high over the heads of the aeronauts, they caught glimpses between and above them of other and different growths, yet higher.

There was no wind in the glade. The sun beat down and the stench rose up. Mr. Jones had a strong feeling that if they did not get out of the place in a short time he was going to be very ill indeed.

"This is awful," he said appealingly. "Can't we go up again?"

The Russian, who had been looking about with much interest, shook his head. "Of what use to rise now when we have just made such a very nice landing? Another time we might not be so lucky. The odor is certainly unpleasant, but after all it is only a smell. It is only the vegetation. I knew that here in the crater valley we would find some very peculiar things. We must not be too easily deterred. Let us penetrate past these vegetables and find what lies beyond."

Sergius undoubtedly had the final say so in regard to their leaving or remaining, so his companion followed his example, unstrapped himself from his seat in the monoplane, and descended to earth. The prince handed him a rifle and cartridge belt and took one himself. They discarded their coats and hoods and advanced toward the nearest passage between the "cabbages."

As they approached the dreadful charnel odor became more intense, if that were possible. Shoulders thrown forward, eyes half-shut and smarting, they pushed through it as through some tangible obstruction.

Then the first of the many-hued mushrooms were crunching beneath their feet. They crushed and squelched, with a semiliquid sound, sending up a sort of acid gas into the faces of the two adventurers, somewhat like the fumes of hydrochloric acid. The prince took out his handkerchief and bound it over his mouth and nose, signaling to Jones to do likewise, for both of them were past speaking. With these improvised and inadequate gas-masks, they waded doggedly on through the fungi.

They were within fifteen feet of one of the smaller cabbages, when with a sort of swishing sound it began to move. Its outer sheath of purple and green leaves, twenty-five feet long and five broad, began to open out and descend.

Jones caught a glimpse between them of a huge, scarlet, writhing mass, and tried to turn and run. The crushed mushroom things held his feet. It was like trying to leap or run in a quicksand.

Then the rough, thick, sawlike edge of the nearest leaf struck him a glancing blow on the shoulder, And he was down in the mess of fungi. A long, writhing, bright-red thing, like a nightmare fishingworm, lashed out above him, curled back and encircled his neck in a strangling grip.

"Help!" he tried to shout. "Sergius—help!"

Then his shoulder was seized and he was being pulled away from the giant cabbage. The tentacle which held him straightened out and actually stretched as if it had been made of india-rubber. A knife flashed over him, severing the tentacle, and a moment later he was out of reach of a dozen more which were shooting after him. That was the last thing he remembered until he came to under the shadow of the plane, to look up into the anxious face of Sergius Petrofsky, who was fanning him with a handkerchief.

Mr. Jones sat up and felt of his neck gingerly. Luckily his collar had somewhat protected it, but it felt very stiff and sore.

"I thought you were gone, my friend," said Sergius, standing up and wiping his perspiring face with the handkerchief.

"So did I. What I can't understand is why the thing didn't get you, too. Look at it now—ugh, the horrible, nasty, writhing beast!"

The "death cabbage" (as they afterward named the interesting vegetables) had not closed its outer sheath, and its inner hideousness stood fully exposed to the sun. Straight up from the center sprang a sort of slimy, blue-black stalk, terminating some twenty-five feet above the ground in a wide plume of green fronds. Surrounding this stalk was a dense, intertwined mass of the long, scarlet tentacles which had nearly dragged Mr. Jones to his doom. To be eaten by a vegetable—and such a vegetable! Jones shuddered and looked away, feeling very sick and disgusted.

"Look!" cried the nihilist. "It is twisting itself about like a thing in agony. I wonder if the brute has eyes and sees us here and still hungers after its prey? But that is curious. See, it is becoming of a bright orange color!"

Jones looked again, rather unwittingly, but what the Russian said was quite true. The wriggling scarlet mass was rapidly changing to orange, and from orange it faded to a sickly yellow. Moreover it was wriggling more and more feebly. The outstretched sheath-leaves lifted themselves spasmodically two or three times, then wilted limply among the fungi at its base. The central stalk began to droop over to one side, and the green fronds hung dispiritedly down. At the end of five minutes all motion had ceased. Even the now pale tentacles writhed no more. The death cabbage was itself dead.

"Do you suppose it perished of a broken heart?" asked Sergius whimsically. "'You resisted its ardent caresses, and it died of disappointment But rather, I think, it possible that another than either of us has killed this monster, my friend."

"What do you mean? Have you seen anybody else?"

Sergius pointed upward solemnly.

"I mean him," he said, and he was pointing at the sun. "There is but one explanation. These are creatures of the night, and they get their—their food in the night, whatever it may be. They are not accustomed to grasp their prey by daylight. This one was tempted, and he opened his protecting sheath, and he was slain by the sun! But he would have killed us first, if I had not been able to spring back more quickly than you, my friend, and escape his first gropings."

"I owe you my life," said Jones earnestly. "I never knew anybody before who would have had the courage to throw himself within reach of that—that thing, and drag another man away from it."

"It is nothing," Sergius demurred, looking very much pleased nevertheless. "Now we will be comrades, indeed—no? I think, however, that we have done and seen enough for one day. Mount again to your seat and we will leave this valley of death. But we will return to-morrow and alight in some more favorable spot."

"I'm with you," Mr. Jones assented joyfully.

But first they cleaned themselves as well as they could of the pulpy fungoids with which they were both plastered; Jones from head-to foot. Then they started to put on their heavy coats. Mr. Jones was buttoning his and Sergius had just slipped his arms into the sleeves, when a voice behind them said sharply: "Stand perfectly still, please! If either one of you moves a finger I'll kill you first, Prince Sergius Petrofsky!"

CHAPTER VII

Startled and amazed, Jones and the nihilist yet obeyed, for there was a certain sincerity back of the command which was not to be denied. Their rifles lay on the ground a few feet distant and Sergius himself, with his arms half into his coat, was peculiarly helpless.

Both looked over their shoulders, however, and there behind them, rifle pointed at the middle of the Russian's back, stood Richard Holloway! He was still attired in his simple costume of shirt and trousers, now very ragged and dirty, and his face wore a grim smile.

"Who are you?" asked Sergius, although he may have guessed.

"It's Holloway," supplied Jones in a whisper.

"You don't need to murmur it in his ear, sweet child," interrupted the newcomer. "I'm so glad to meet you again, Rolly. You know I said I was sure we should be friends. But we thought after all a stalactite must have dropped and crushed out your innocent young life."

Mr. Jones could think of no reply. Of course, now, the other party would never believe that he had not been lying when he said that he had nothing to do with Sergius Petrofsky. Even Jim Haskins would no longer believe him. Then he forgot his own troubles in wondering how this unexpected meeting would affect his newer friend, Sergius.

"Move farther back from those rifles," commanded Holloway. "That's right. And just remember that I don't love either of you one little bit. The only pity is that my dear little vegetable garden didn't succeed in getting both of you for its luncheon. It's a lucky thing for you that you didn't try conclusions with one of the really big fellows. That one was a mere child—poor innocent thing!" He shifted his rifle to the hollow of his arm and came toward them.

Sergius, his face white and strained with anger, still stood with his arms half way in the coat. "May I—have I your very kind permission, Mr. Holloway, to finish putting on my coat? I give you my word that we are neither of us armed, except for the rifles."

"In just a minute, prince. Sorry about your word, but if you did happen to get careless about it, where would I be? Rolly, I've got you covered. Just go over and turn your friend's pockets inside out for me, will you? And now your own? That's right. No, I wronged your serene highness. You can put your coat on, though you must be a cold-blooded fish to want it in this sun."

"We were just about to ascend," said the Russian stiffly.

"Oh, I see. Well, you're just about not to ascend now, so you won't need it. We saw you fluttering gaily about over the valley, and saw you drop into this place. Paul (he really seems to retain a regard for you, for some reason), your brother, asked me to come out and pick up the remains, if there were any, which I doubted myself, knowing what sort of place you had landed in. He asked me to extend to you his apologies for not coming himself. He sprained his ankle in the caves, but Miss Weston is looking after him so well that really it can't be much hardship."

Sergius' eyes narrowed, and Jones remembered that Jim Haskins had told him both brothers were seeking the girl's favor.

Holloway picked up the two rifles from the ground and tucked them under his other arm. "So nice of you," he murmured. "We're rather short on arms and ammunition. But I know you're anxious to be welcomed in camp. Turn to the right, please, and straight ahead. Don't be frightened of the little cabbages. I won't feed you to them this time."

Jones was beginning to detest the young American as much as he had formerly been inclined to like him. His mocking banter in this place that smelt like the tomb and was the home of detestable death, seemed as out of place as the tinkle of a pianola in Purgatory.

However, the man must know a safe way out, or he could not have appeared there himself, so the two prisoners turned their faces in the direction indicated and started off, with Holloway close behind.

They crossed the glade obliquely and came into view of a broad road, or trail, which had apparently been trampled over and through the fungi and several of the young and comparatively small death plants which lay crushed and broken. Two of them, each well above ten feet from root to crest, had been actually torn up by the roots and tossed to some distance from the place where they had been growing.

What power or agency had been strong enough to perform such a feat with such victims?

As they involuntarily paused, staring, Holloway's mocking voice answered the unspoken question:

"That's the work of another of my lovely island's children. Don't get scared. He doesn't prowl around much by daylight, but when he does take a walk, and things get in his way or annoy him, he just pushes them gently to one side—as you see. He's a foul brute, but not foul enough to feed upon such carrion plants as these. He was probably hunting something."

The nihilist was too proud, and Jones too overcome, to question Holloway in regard to the mysterious "brute" to which he referred, and after a moment of hesitation they marched on through the sickening mess of broken fungi and wilted, blood-sucking tentacles. But first, at Holloway's own suggestion, they all three again bound handkerchiefs over mouth and nose as a partial protection against the thrice-vile fumes rising from beneath their feet.

At last, however, a breath of purer air reached their nostrils, and raising his head, Jones's watering eyes beheld a scene of weird and unearthly beauty. Behind them lay the field of death cabbages, in all its foul ugliness. Before them was a forest—but such a forest! The trees were mere slender, graceful stems, shooting up to an unbelievable height, where they branched out into a feathery tuft of graceful leaves, resembling palms.

But these slender stems were all wound and garlanded with gorgeous blossoms, like glorious floral butterflies swaying and fluttering to every breath of air.

Here and there huge balloonlike growths had forced their way upward between the palms, bending them aside and so making their own path to the sunlight. These, however, unlike the cabbages, had nothing horrible or loathsome in their appearance, but were of the most delicate shades of pink, shading into lemon yellow at the summits. They, too, were overgrown in the riotous embrace of a thousand blossoming vines.

Underfoot the ground was thickly carpeted with moss in wide patches, like rich rugs of velvet green, starred all over with little points of brilliant blue and scarlet, which were also flowers. Between the butterflylike blossoms of the vines innumerable real butterflies were flitting. Their colors were so similar to the flowers that it was impossible to tell if a blossom one's eyes rested upon were really such or a butterfly, unless it suddenly spread its wings and flickered away through the slanting sunlight.

Moving forward slowly, like men in a dream of fairyland, they came at last entirely out of the zone of vile odors; and the more delightful by contrast, their nostrils were filled by the divine fragrance of this unlegended Garden of the Hesperides.

Again Holloway had his comment to make.

"You like this all right, now—but I just invite you to take the trip by moonlight!"

"By moonlight," said the Russian softly, forgetting for the moment his animosity toward the speaker. "I should think by moonlight this place would be—ah, celestial!

"H—m! Well, I've been here, and take it from me it was more like the other place."

"Impossible!

"In the bright lexicon of Joker Island, there ain't no such word, dear child. Your imagination needs exercise—or you wouldn't have come here, so I'll just permit you to exercise it on this. But I'll give you one tip: You've seen the flora, but you haven't seen the fauna—yet. Straight ahead, now, through that little lane between the vegetable balloons. No, not that way. Halt! Good Lord, man, if you'd gone down there you'd have wished you was safe inside one of those mild-tempered little cabbages back yonder!"

Sergius, absorbed in gazing at the wonders about them, had started to go to the left of the balloon in question instead of the right. The ground sloped sharply downward there, and as he drew back his foot in surprise at Holloway's evident agitation, there was a sudden rattle and slide off falling gravel.

Both he and his fellow-captive looked keenly down the incline, but could see nothing out of the way. A tangle of gray, leafless vines formed a veil across the bottom of the slope, through which they could see nothing.

Then, the perspiration sprang out on Sergius' forehead, and for the first time since Jones had met him the prince looked really frightened. For over that tangle of vines something was moving. It was a leg, and it had come out from between the vines. It was jointed in two places, the space between the upper joints being about three feet long, and at the end of it was a single, great, curved claw, black and gleaming like polished ebony.

Another similar leg followed it into visibility. Then two eyes came into view, round, black, and fastened upon the ends of stalks like those of a lobster.

"Good God!" breathed the Russian.

"What is the thing, Holloway?"

"Just a. little spider," responded their captor cheerfully. "But plenty big enough to make three mouthfuls of you. That's its web it's sitting in, wondering why you don't come on down to dinner. I'd shoot the old devil, but what's the use? He's only one. Shall we go on now?"

With cold shivers running up and down their spinal columns, Mr. Jones and his companion stepped carefully back from the entrance to the giant spider's den, and entered a little path or trail which led windingly away through the lovely, treacherous forest. Jones, for one, heartily wished that their guardian would march in front instead of the rear. The death cabbages had been bad enough, but they had seemed such vast, unnatural prodigies that already his memory reproduced them dreamily.

That spider was another matter. He had, heard of spiders as large as dinner plates, and shuddered at the thought of them. This spider had been as large as well, judging from its forelegs it could better be compared with an extra large dining-table.

And Holloway had spoken of it as "only one." How many more such fiends lay hidden, waiting for the false tread of a foot, or the careless speed of some hunted jungle thing? He began to be careful indeed to look where he trod, and suspicious of even the supposedly harmless flowers and butterflies. Beauty becomes more horrible than frank ugliness when one has learned that death lurks behind it.

Fortunately, however, for their peace of mind they saw no more of the "fauna" of which Holloway had hinted, although once in skirting a dark morass they heard distant crashing sounds, as if some large beast were threshing about somewhere in the depths.

"This place is like a Broadway cafe," Holloway informed them. "Nothing much doing in the daytime— but—oh you midnight suppers. Eat and be eaten, that's our motto after sunset."

"You seem to know a whole lot about the place," Jones ventured.

"Yes, indeed. Regular old homestead to little Willy. You see, I lived here for two years, and got real well acquainted with the inhabitants. Maybe we'll let you and your dear friend Prince Sergius try it, when it comes time for us to leave. You'd learn a whole lot you never knew before, believe me. That is, if you survived the first week or two."

Mr. Jones looked at him hopelessly. Was the man in earnest?

But Sergius laughed scornfully. "I should not particularly mind," he said, "so long as we were relieved of your company, Mr. Holloway."

"You don't say! How very rude and unkind you are, prince. But never mind. I'd be sore, too, if I were in your place, so I forgive you like a true Christian. And here we are—home at last all safe and sound."

For the path, turning sharply, passed out of the jungle and into the full light of day. Half a mile away, across a broad expanse of green meadow, the rim of the crater raised its black height, hidden from them until now by the forest. To the right, in the distance, some unidentifiable animals were grazing, and ahead, close to the wall, a pillar of smoke was rising, almost white against its dead blackness.

"There's our camp. Keep right on going. Don't worry, they're expecting us."

That they were expected was presently evidenced, for the figure of a man appeared coming toward them across the meadow. In a few minutes Jones was able to identify him, for it was Jim, Paul's cowboy retainer. He met then, with a grin, which suddenly faded as he recognized Mr. Jones. He looked from him to Sergius and then back again.

"Well, of all the—snakes!" he exclaimed, and his hand dropped suggestively to his hip-pocket. "So that yarn of yours was just a string of whoppers, was it? By jiminy, I've a notion to drill you right now, you—you low-down horsethief! Lettin' me get the notion that you was layin' smashed back there in the cave, and me mad as thunder because they wouldn't let me hike back to look for you. An' all the time you pikin' around with this here nihilanarchist bunch. Say, what kind of a low-down, lyin' cattle-rustler are you, anyhow?"

"Shut up, Jimmy," interrupted Holloway at last, although he had listened to the arraignment with a grin of pure enjoyment. "Rolly's nerves are all upset as it is. How is Prince Petrofsky?"

Jim's face relaxed again into a grin.

"Doin' fine," he answered. "I know now why he brought that female woman along. Gee! I wouldn't mind sprainin' a leg or so to get nursed that luxurious."

"He'll get well for pure joy when he sees who's here. Forward the army. We'll be right behind you, gentlemen. Sorry the hotel bus wasn't running, so as to save your walking all this way, but you know what these summer resorts are."

His cheerful nonsense bored Jones wretchedly, as they went on toward the camp. What sort of a greeting were he and Sergius likely to get? Not a very pleasant one, judging from the sample offered by Haskins. He heartily wised that Sergius had stuck to his original intention of "a mere reconnaissance." They would have been back with the nihilists by this time, and at that moment the nihilist camp actually seemed like home to Mr. Jones.

What could there possibly be in the crater valley of sufficient value to make all these people so very anxious to reach it? Unless the were seeking the rather morbid pleasure of being killed and eaten, he could conceive of nothing liable to be there which would repay the extreme trouble and risk attendant upon obtaining it.

A gold mine? How could anybody work a gold mine in a place like this? Diamonds, perhaps? He himself would have cheerfully forfeited a full ownership in Tiffany's just to escape from the place.

He had never had any opportunity to question Sergius Petrofsky, and as that gentleman stalked along moodily by his side now he did not look in a good humor to answer such interrogations. Both men had long since removed their heavy coats and were carrying them, but even-so their clothing was saturated with perspiration.

Hot, weary, and disgusted, they neither of them looked as they came into camp, as if they had been upon any pleasurable expedition.

A fire was snapping and crackling cheerfully in the cliff shadow, and about it lay scattered various paraphernalia, but no one was in sight.

"All in the cave," said Jim, in an explanatory tone. "Some cliff-dwellers, our bunch, ain't we, Holloway?"

"First-class apartments," corrected the other. "Dry, airy, cool, but dogs and children barred. Hey, there! Anybody home?"

At Holloway's hail a woman appeared in the entrance to one of a large number of the dark openings which perforated the crater wall. It was of course Margaret Weston.

"Oh, did you find them, Mr. Holloway? Who is that with the prince? Isn't that the man we lost in the caverns?"

"It sure is, ma'am," grinned the cowboy, not giving Holloway a chance to reply. "He ain't crushed none, not so you could notice it. I take off my hat to you, ma'am. You was dead right about the snake, but I was too plumb pigheaded to know it."

"That is all right, James," said the girl, smiling sweetly. "A woman's intuition is sometimes correct after all, is it not? Prince Sergius," with a sudden severe formality, "your brother would like to see you as soon as it is convenient."

The nihilist bowed with a dignity equal to her own. His face was sternly set, but Jones, watching curiously, saw a look flash up into his eyes as they rested on the girl which confirmed the cowboy's statement in regard to his feeling toward her. He could hardly be blamed, either. Miss Weston looked a good deal more than attractive, standing there with one white, shapely arm extended to support herself on the precarious foothold of rocks at the cavern door. She looked very young, girlish and utterly out of place in that nightmare valley. Her smooth cheeks were slightly flushed, her scarlet lips were set just sufficiently to bring out their exquisite lines, and her big blue eyes were shining with some emotion, but one hardly favorable to Sergius, if Mr. Jones were any judge.

In fact, Miss Weston was angry, and Jones felt vaguely sorry for Sergius Petrofsky. He wondered again at the girl's ardent dislike for his friend.

"I am grateful to my brother," said Sergius slowly, "for sending such a charming messenger!"

"Thank you. But kindly reserve your compliments for some one who will better deserve and—appreciate them. Mr. Holloway, will you kindly accompany these gentlemen? The sailors are in the other cave, and I hardly think it safe for Prince Paul to receive them alone—"

Sergius flushed deeply. The thrust evidently went home.

"Certainly, Miss Weston," assented Holloway, with a smile of amusement. "But I was just going to start cooking supper."

"I am not myself such a bad cook as you seem to think," laughed the girl. "What use is a woman in camp if she can't do the nursing and cooking?"

"You're dead right, ma'am," commented Jim, but in a most respectful voice. Jones reflected sadly that even this woman-hater appeared to have been converted to admiration for the girl. Probably he regarded her diagnosis of his, Jones's, character as a symptom of most unusual wisdom.

"Go right in, gentlemen," commanded Holloway. "Here, Jim, will you take these rifles? And lend me your little popgun? Thanks. A rifle is no good at close quarters."

With a disdainful shrug Sergius turned his back on the voluble American and entered the cave, Mr. Jones close at his heels.

CHAPTER VIII

On one of the dark but cool chambers in the rock a rude couch of blankets had been laid. Beside it, upon a flat-topped stone, stood an electric lantern of the type which, using large batteries, will burn for eighty or ninety hours, and which illuminated the place quite brightly. Beside it a bottle of arnica and some carefully folded bandages were arranged.

Upon the couch lay Paul Petrofsky, the lower part of one leg swathed in more and beautifully adjusted bandages. As the two captives entered, however, he sat up and gave utterance to an exclamation of joy as he recognized his brother.

For the first time, seeing them together, Jones realized the strong resemblance between the two men. There were the same broad, intelligent brow, the same high-bridged, symmetrical nose, the same thin-lipped, sensitive mouth, and pleasant, dark eyes. The only real difference between the two faces lay in the expression and in that slight inclination of Paul's chin to recede.

Sergius' eyes were keen as well as pleasant, his mouth was set in firmer lines, and his chin was of a squarish and very determined shape. Also, at time, his face wore a haughty and somewhat domineering look—a look which Paul's countenance never assumed.

If, knowing neither of them, Jones had been asked to choose, he would have unhesitatingly named Sergius as the supporter of aristocratic government, and Paul as the man to be easily led, particularly into any scheme, however wild, for the betterment of his fellow Russians.

"Sergius!" exclaimed the man on the couch. There was pure relief in his voice. "Then you are safe. I was afraid—"

"That some of your friend Holloway's pets had made a meal an your dear brother? I should not have thought that would have appeared to you as a great trouble, Paul."

His brother shook his head impatiently, with a slight frown.

"That is absurd, as you very well know. Because you have been misled by these murderous, bomb-throwing companions of yours is no reason for me to forget that you are my brother."

Sergius flushed and straightened himself.

"My companions are not bomb-throwers, and you very well know the difference between nihilism and the madness of anarchy, although you choose to pretend that there is none. You are in a position to say what you please to me, Paul, but you know my feelings on that subject and it seems hardly generous—"

"It is not a question of generosity, but of common sense," the other broke out. "Someday you will thank me for standing out against your fanatical views. Russia will never be saved by such mad dreamers as your so-called friends. It is I who truly serve Russia in her hour of need. How long, think you, will the war which is slaughtering our people continue after I turn over to the government the—that which we have come to seek?"

"Long enough, I hope, to destroy every member of the cruel beaurocracy which holds her in its bloody grip. Yes, it is your friends who are bloody, Paul, not mine."

"There is tyranny in every fixed government. Moreover, it is not the rulers of Russia who suffer most. It is the very peasantry which you profess to love so much. Turn your face from the mirage you are pursuing, my brother, and cast in your lot with us!"

"I will not desert my brothers," replied Sergius briefly, but with evident sincerity.

"Then," said Prince Paul with some firmness, "you will not be allowed to return to them either. Dick Holloway, I had hoped that after all I might persuade my brother—I have no brothers—to ally himself with us. Since he is not yet ready to do so, I must ask that you and James Haskins see to it that he remains in this camp. As for his companion, the spy, it would be no more than right if we should shoot him outright."

Jones started slightly, This amiable-looking Russian seemed to be even more arbitrary than his nihilist brother.

"Oh, I wouldn't go that far," counseled Holloway, with an amused grin. "I'll be responsible for it that—he doesn't leave us so easily as he did before. By the way, prince, I left the aeroplane where they landed. Do you want the thing brought into camp?"

"No, I think not," said Paul, after a moment's hesitation. "I fail to see how it could be of any use to us. If you or Jim chance to go that way again you might see to it that it is rendered useless for any one, however." He gave a significant glance in the direction of the plane's rightful owner.

Then he dropped back upon his couch with a little grimace of pain. "Sergius, will you remain here with me? I should very much like to hear of what befell when you descended into the valley. That is, if you don't mind telling me. Dick Holloway, please take this man Jones out with you and set him to work about the camp. We may as well make him useful since you are set on keeping him."

Holloway looked doubtfully at the two brothers. Sergius saw the look and laughed bitterly.

"You had better assure your friend, Paul, that I am unlikely to murder you in his absence. Also you are mistaken in regard to Mr. Jones's relations with me. I never met the gentleman until night before last, and we parted then because he managed to cut a hole in the side of his prison tent and escape. I will admit that I do now regard him as a friend, but that is because of his very excellent qualities. We are friends, however, and any treatment which you accord him I must beg you to offer me also."

He looked very haughty and dignified as he uttered these sentiments, and Mr. Jones's heart went out to him more than ever. The man had not only saved his life, but now he was defending him from undeserved oppression. Somehow, he determined, he would endeavor to repay Prince Sergius.

Paul shrugged his shoulders and smiled rather dubiously at his brother. "' Of course, if you say he did not come to our camp as a spy I shall have to take your word. You are in a position to know if any one is. Holloway, we will have to treat the gentleman courteously, since my brother is determined to share his fate." He laughed. "I really don't care to make you wash dishes Sergius."

Holloway and Mr. Jones went back to the camp fire, leaving the two brothers alone together. There was no exit to the cavern chamber, save that by which they had entered, and even Holloway did not really believe that the nihilist would harm his brother for mere revenge.

Jones longed to ask some questions in regard to this mysterious war which had been again hinted at, but he still suffered from a deep-seated dread of what the answer might reveal, and also of being regarded by these strangers as hopelessly feeble-minded.

"Let it wait. If I'm really crazy I'm bound to find it out soon enough," he thought bitterly.

In a short time supper was prepared, consisting of canned goods and the fresh meat of some animal, probably one of those creatures which still grazed quietly in the distant meadow. Jones, for one, was ravenously hungry. He had eaten nothing save the bowl of stew brought him by Doherty for thirty-six hours or more, and did full justice to Miss Weston's cooking, which was excellent. She explained this by saying that she had taken a course in domestic science to supplement a brief hospital training, preparatory to her work as a Red Cross nurse in the European battlefields.

The European battlefields! How much of Europe then was involved in this mad, chimerical war of theirs? Whoever the fighters might be, he felt that they had missed a very beautiful and determined young nurse when Miss Weston was sidetracked into this equally mad island affair. Mr. Jones was feeling more and more as if, having slept a single night, he had awakened into a new and entirely unfamiliar world.

Paul had managed to hobble out of his cavern retreat, supporting himself on the shoulder of his brother, and the whole party, including the two sailors, ate together without regard to caste or rank. Paul was glad to sit down at once, but Sergius first wandered about for a few moments, apparently inspecting the arrangements. Jones wondered if his reckless companion had designs on the rifles, three of which lay together close by; but if this were so he resigned them as impracticable, for presently he came and seated himself between Holloway and his brother.

As he did so he leaned across, behind Holloway's back, and whispered something to Jones, who had taken his place just beyond. Jones, however, did not catch the words, and he thought best not to attract the attention of the company by asking for a repetition.

The upper rim of the sun was just disappearing below the western wall as they finished, and only a few minutes later the sudden tropic night was upon them, with its wonderful stars and refreshing, fragrant breath of coolness.

It brought something more than coolness in its wake, it brought a rising wave of sound from the jungle beyond the open meadow. The valley of the day was no more, and the valley of night had swung wide its doors for all the creatures which crouched, awaiting the liberating touch of darkness.

The first intimation of this other valley, which none of the party save Holloway really knew, was a deep-throated roar from the jungle immediately opposite. This was followed by a sort of wild, bubbling shriek, as of a creature slivering from nightmare. The sound ended so abruptly that one could only judge the shrieker to have been swallowed by the roarer. Next there was a great snarling and yowling and crashing of branches, as if two enormous tom-cats were engaged in a combat to the death. The noise of battle was soon drowned out, however, by the full rising chorus of night life, the separate notes of which, all blended as into one mighty, discordant cry, rising harshly toward the white, indifferent stars.

Only Holloway remained entirely unaffected by the uproar. Miss Weston, the intrepid, actually trembled and shrank toward the protecting of her Russian lover—that is, of the Russian lover she favored.

The two sailors sprang to their feet and looked longingly in the direction of the caverns. Arizona Jim reached casually over and drew his rifle up beside him. Sergius also gazed desirefully in the direction of the rifles, forbidden to him and Jones, while the latter, shuddering inwardly, remembered that they had actually walked through the midst of all that only a couple of hours ago.

"Some opera, isn't it?" remarked Holloway, with an amused glance about the little circle of white faces. "When I first came here I used to lie all night and shiver and shake and try to make up sleep in the daytime. I had a gun, but only a little ammunition, you know. I found that a good-sized fire would keep all but the really big fellows away, though, so I got in the habit of building one in front of a small cave and sleeping behind it. If a little fellow came along, he was afraid of the fire. A big one couldn't get in the cave. Great Scott! For a while after I got taken off the island I couldn't sleep at all. Missed the noise, you see."

"Great Heaven! What was that?"

The whole party, except Holloway, sprang to their feet and stared wildly into the air. Something huge, black, monstrous had flapped out of the darkness and into it again, passing so close that the wind of its flight scattered burning brands right and left from the fire.

"Guess we'd better be going to bed," said Holloway, rising but with no undue haste. "I don't know exactly what those things are, because I've never caught a glimpse of the brutes by daylight, but the fire really seems to attract them instead of keeping them away. Once one of 'em made a grab at me in passing. Made a nasty gash on my cheek. I just dodged into my little boudoir in time."

"It looked like a—like a great, impossible bat," cried Margaret Weston, and there was a hysterical note in her voice. "Oh, why was I brought to this frightful place? Why did we not retire into the caverns before sunset, as we did last night?"

"Poor little girl," said Paul Petrofsky gently. "I never would have brought you here, if there had been any other way. Come. You shall sleep to-night on that nice, soft couch you prepared for me, Miss Margaret, and Dick Holloway and I will sleep in the cave entrance. Nothing shall come near you that can harm."

"There's really no need for you to be frightened," interrupted Holloway in a more serious and considerate tone than one usually heard from his lips. "There are five men of us, at least, who are well-armed, and any one of us would die before we would let harm come to the only girl in Joker Island."

Sergius bit his lip, but said nothing. By his "five men" the American had carefully left him and Mr. Jones out of the number of Miss Weston's protectors.

"You and Rolly," continued Holloway, addressing the nihilist, "can sleep in Room 5, Suite A. Here it is, and here's a torch. Be sparing with it, for we haven't many more batteries."

He pointed out the cave which he humorously dignified with the title of Room 5. "Jimmy boy will be right at your door in case you want anything in the night," he added significantly.

The prisoners entered, Sergius leading the way with the torch. They found it to be a small but dry cavern, and as they spread down their heavy coats to sleep on, it seemed as decent a bedroom as could be expected. It also formed a very efficient jail, since, like the other where Paul had lain, it had but the one exit, and that way led past the presumably wakeful Jim Haskins.

At least he had enough to keep him awake in listening to the wild night chorus of Joker Island and keeping his little fire going at the entrance.

For a time the two companions in misfortune lay silent, listening to the uproar which was somewhat muffled by the rocky walls about them. It was Jones who spoke first, voicing a question which had been all along in his mind.

"Prince Sergius," he said, "what on earth are you and the rest of them after in this place? I mean, why did Holloway want to come back, and why did he persuade your brother to fit out a yacht and come after him, and why did you—" He paused suddenly, wondering just how sensitive the prince was on that subject.

But his companion laughed softly in the darkness.

"That American—that Jim—he did not tell you everything, eh?"

"I think he told me all he knew. But of course, if you don't want to trust me, just say so. I'm only curious, that's all."

"But I do trust you." Sergius reached over, caught Jones's hand, gripped it hard, and then dropped it as suddenly. "Really—do not laugh—you are the only friend I have within two thousand miles at least. Those men of mine? They are of the rough peasant type whom I pity but cannot love. My Captain Ivanovitch? He is—well, to be frank, I do not like him. He has not the least refinement. My brother? Ah, yes, I love him, but we are not friends—not now. He is my elder, the head of my house since our father died.

"Paul was educated in America, and our father sent me to Oxford, for he was a man of broad, splendid ideas. He thought thus we two should share the education of two continents, but instead it was so we grew apart. At Oxford I met other Russians, thinking men, one of whom—alas, he is now in Siberia—changed the whole course of my life. But I cannot now tell you of all that. Paul, in your free America, clung still to the old, I call them the cruel and tyrannous, ideals.

"But you I liked, even when I thought you were that beast, Richard Holloway. It is true that I threatened you, but then I was angry, because I wished you to do something reasonable and you would not. But when we met again and I asked you to come with me into this place of hell, you did not even hesitate. You came like an old friend—a comrade."

"But you saved my life afterward, prince," said Jones, amazed at this tribute and the evidently sincere feeling which lay behind it. "I am in your debt for that and for standing up for me to your brother."

"And why not? Comrades must not desert one another. And I do not like to be named prince. Such titles stand for all I most abhor, Call me Sergius and I will call you Roland, as friends should. Tell me, would you go yet further and accompany me upon a greater adventure than any of these dogs that hold us dare attempt?"

"What do you mean?" asked Mr. Jones, somewhat startled.

"I mean," the other replied, lowering his voice to a whisper, "that to-morrow they will destroy our only means of escape—the aeroplane. To-night it still stands there, safe unless some night-devil has trampled it. In half an hour we could be on board the Monterey. Is it not worth some risk to attain that? And we could return, but next time we would not be trapped so easily. We would be upon our guard."

"Good Lord," groaned Mr. Jones. "What you propose is impossible, prince—I mean, Sergius. We should be killed before we had gone fifty yards into that nightmare out there."

"You hesitate? But I have not yet answered your question. Listen. In this island—this island which contains so many strange and unaccountable surprises—in its soil is a substance more valuable a thousand times than gold."

"Radium?" hazarded Mr. Jones.

"Radium—bah! No, it is a strange, secret substance, which for ages has been sought by science until it has been termed a vision of fools and madmen." He lowered his voice yet more. "It is that which was once named the Philosopher's Stone—and it will change the nature of what have been called the elements. My friend, this substance will transmute common lead to gold!"

"Oh, is that all?" sighed Mr. Jones. "I thought it was probably something about gold, but believe me, it isn't worth it, prince—it really isn't."

Sergius sat up, and Jones knew that he was staring at him in amazement.

"You are a very strange man, my friend. Has gold no temptation for you?"

"Not a bit—not that sort of gold, anyway. Do you realize that if this mythical stuff of Holloway's proves what he has claimed to you people, it will upset the financial systems of the entire world, and become itself of no more value than—than mud?"

"Not at all. Do you think we would be so mad as to flood the world with gold? No, we will give out that we have discovered a very valuable mine and we will only release it in such quantities as may prove judicious. For myself, I desire it only for the cause. Russia shall be freed from herself and become a blazing lamp of liberty to enlighten the whole world. Paul, he desires only to help the government in overcoming the Germans. I desire to make the Germans my brothers."

So, it was really Germany that Russia was fighting! It all seemed very strange. If it had been England, now—

"As for this Holloway," continued Sergius, "who discovered it, he thinks only of himself. He says he wants to be a captain of industry."

"But why didn't he bring some of the stuff away with him in the first place?"

"He could carry only a little, and that was used up in demonstrating to us its value. But there is a great deal more here—the whole soil is impregnated with it, and he discovered it by the chance of a leaden bullet falling into the fire. The heat melted the bullet and it sank to the earth beneath. And in the morning, when he swept away the ashes from before his cave, there lay a splash of gold upon the ground. He is a bright man, this Richard Holloway, and after thought he experimented with another bullet."

"Yes, he would," sighed Mr. Jones in spite of Sergius' assurance, the effect on himself and all his friends, if this improbable tale proved true, was staggering to contemplate. "Now I know why I dislike the man so much. Isn't the air in here frightfully stuffy? I can hardly keep my eyes open."

"A little smoke from the fire at the entrance, perhaps. Or—my friend, do not tell me that you ignored the warning I gave you!"

"Warning? What warning?" Jones felt himself growing drowsier and drowsier. He wished Sergius would shut up and let him sleep.

He realized that some one was shaking him vigorously. "The soup—the tomato soup! Tell me, surely you did not eat of it?"

"Yes—sure. Good soup. Mighty nice soup—nice girl—too—"

His voice dwindled away. He was drifting comfortably off upon a sea of the softest down. Then something hard, unpleasant, was thrusting itself against his teeth. His mouth filled with fire-liquid fire. Coughing, strangling, he sat up and recovered sufficiently to push his companion's hand away from his mouth.

"Wha'—wha' you tryin' to do?" he asked hoarsely. His throat and lips felt stiff and numb.

"Trying to revive you, my friend. Here, drink some more of this."

"No. 'S horrid stuff. Take—away."

"Drink. You must."

Again something was forced against his teeth in the dark, and his mouth was flooded with the fiery liquid.

It was "horrid stuff," but it was effective. Jones felt the numbness going out of his vocal organs, and his brain cleared.

"What's the matter with me?" he gasped. "Have I been poisoned?"

"No, no, just a harmless drug, but it would have been disastrous had you succumbed to it, though I pray Heaven the rest have done so. I warned you not to touch that soup. Why did you do it?"

"Was that what you whispered to me? I didn't understand. But do you mean to tell me that you have—that you have—"

"I've put them all to sleep, that's all. The stuff is a perfectly harmless soporific, but it tastes a little, and that is why I put it in the highly seasoned soup, which all would be most likely to eat. But it is fortunate I had with me also the antidote, or my plan would have surely reacted upon myself, for I would not leave you here to meet their anger."

Jones staggered to his feet.

"I can't say I like the idea, my friend, but I suppose from your point of view you were justified. What are we to do now?"

"Get back to the aeroplane. It is useless for us to attempt the cavern without a guide, and even if I could awaken Holloway, I doubt if he could be induced to help us."

"You would leave them here—in a drugged sleep—defenceless? Why man what are you thinking of? It would be worse than murder! And the girl, too. Why, the idea is criminal!"

"For what sort of devil do you mistake me, Roland Jones? No, I have thought of everything. We will place them all in the cavern chamber where Miss Weston now lies. Then we will block, up the entrance with large stones, build before it a great fire, and they will certainly be as safe until morning as anyone can be in this perilous place."

"I see. Well, perhaps it could be done. But first, hadn't we better find out if every one is really asleep?"

CHAPTER IX

Having first lighted the electric torch, the two men crept stealthily through the narrow passage. In the doorway the fire had burned low, and beside it lay sprawled the figure of Jim Haskins. The nihilist stooped over him and felt cautiously of his heart. Then he straightened himself. "All right," he murmured, and they passed on out. At each of the two other inhabited caves they made a similar examination, and in every case Sergius' little dose had done its work. Every one of their captors lay helpless.

"Let us begin with Paul," said Sergius, in his natural voice, since no need of caution seemed to now exist. But he received an unexpected reply. There was a sudden rustling, a sound of footsteps, and there behind Paul's outstretched form appeared a slender figure.

"You here!" exclaimed Miss Weston. "What have you done to Paul? Have you killed him? Oh, you—you anarchist!"

She dropped on her knees and felt anxiously for Paul's heart.

"My dear Miss Weston, certainly I have not killed my brother." Sergius' voice showed not the slightest agitation at this discovery by the girl he so much admired. "He is only asleep. They are all asleep. We grew tired of seeing so many people asleep, and we are therefore about to leave."

She sprang up and faced him with flushed cheeks and blazing eyes. "You have drugged them all! How did you accomplish this dastardly thing?"

"The tomato soup, Miss Weston. You did not eat of it?"

"Of course not. I detest canned tomato soup. Well, I—I hope you are proud of yourself. I hope—I hope something will eat you! So, you were going away, leaving your brother and all of us to be killed, were you?"

"By no means. We were just about to provide against that little contingency. But your being awake alters matters."

"Oh, does it? Perhaps you are ashamed of your work, now that a woman has seen you at it?"

"Not at all. But on the other hand, I cannot leave you here, awake, to be terrorized all night. Asleep, it would not have mattered. When you awoke it would have been daylight and the others would have also awakened with you. Mr. Jones, the aeroplane will easily carry three passengers. We will have to take Miss Weston with us."

"Oh, I say," protested Jones, "do you think that is really necessary?"

"But yes. She will be far safer on the Monterey than here, under any circumstances. You need not fear me, Miss Weston. I am a gentleman and Paul's brother, when we have settled our brotherly differences, you may return to his side, if that is your choice."

He looked at her a trifle appealingly, but she flung back her head defiantly.

"You dare!" she stormed. "I will not go a step and leave my friends to be devoured."

Sergius took one stride across the body of his brother and seized the young lady in his arms, holding her firmly, but as gently as he could. She did not scream, but she fought desperately, and with an amazing strength.

Jones's gorge rose at the sight. This was going much too far. He sprang forward and seized his companion by the shoulder.

"Here, this won't do," he exclaimed. "You can't force the young lady in that way, Sergius."

The Russian turned a disgusted face to him and said over his shoulder, "Do you prefer to leave her here to be frightened into insanity? Is that your idea of chivalry?"

"Let me go—let me go!" cried Miss Weston, beating fiercely at him with her hands.

And just at that moment something black, monstrous, hideous shot down upon them out of the blackness beyond the fires. There was a harsh, grating scream, and the shoulder of a giant wing struck Jones, knocking him down, and grazed the rock wall. He was involved in a swirl of beating, struggling pinions, there were two more screams, one human, the other quite the opposite, and the thing, whatever it was, was gone.

Jones picked himself up, bruised and trembling from head to foot. The girl lay limp in Sergius' arms, her face white, arms and head hanging. Sergius himself was pale as a ghost, but he had not moved from his position.

"I don't know what it was, Roland Jones," he said with a rather stiff-lipped smile, "but do you still think we ought to leave her here?"

"Great Heavens, how can we take her? How can we go ourselves? Sergius Petrofsky, I believe that you have gone mad!"

"Not quite," said the prince patiently. "We have the rifles and the electric torches, and I really believe we can make the trip safely. I have myself passed through an African jungle in the same way, and never received a scratch. We will carry Miss Weston as far as the outer edge of the meadow, then we will revive her and go on. Later we will open negotiations with my brother—he will not then have so much advantage—and Miss Weston, for whom I have great reverence and respect, will be far safer on the

Monterey. Come! In the midst of so many perils, the boldest course is best. You say that I saved your life. It was a very ordinary deed, but for this one night let me claim your gratitude!"

Jones was in a quandary. His innate chivalry revolted at the idea of forcing a woman into accompanying them, yet the arguments of Sergius seemed very plausible. And he loved this daring, fanatical, imperious new friend of his as he had never loved any man in his life before.

"All right. I'll do it. But afterward Miss Weston is to be free to return here if she chooses."

"Very well, if you wish it. I give my word."

With no more talk they hastily dragged the insensible members of the party into the selected cavern, and with considerable labor blocked up the entrance. In the morning the imprisoned ones could easily pull it down from within. Then they gathered all the fuel together and made one enormous bonfire, that blazed and roared skyward. Some of the logs were of very satisfactory size, and they felt sure the fire would burn for some hours. It was then nearly midnight and dawn would break shortly after three.

While they worked Jones found himself casting many apprehensive glances upward, but the flying monster did not return and they completed their task unmolested. Miss Weston, fortunately or otherwise, had not awakened from her swoon.

Their own two rifles and ammunition belts, together with an automatic pistol and cartridge clips belonging to Prince Paul, and a heavy, old-fashioned revolver looted from Jim Haskins, they had kept outside the cavern, together with two of the most powerful electric torches.

With one last anxious glance skyward, Mr. Jones picked up the two rifles, both torches and their heavy coats, which he was to carry until they reached the place where Sergius' remarkable scheme involved reviving the fainting lady. Sergius himself carefully raised his scornful idol in two muscular arms, and so burdened they started out across the meadow.

How they were to find their way along that thread-like trail, between the hidden dens of impossibly large spiders and past the other roaring, screaming, bellowing natives of Joker Island, remained to be shown.

CHAPTER X

They had reached the first of the scattered outer sentinels of the forest of slender palms. Dimly beyond it, by grace of the tropic star brilliance, they could see the looming mass which they must penetrate to reach the aeroplane.

So far they had met with nothing alarming. Everywhere, in and out, giant fireflies danced in a mystic saraband, very beautiful to behold, but also quite confusing to the eye. They had not yet used their torches, fearing to attract more of the terrible flying monsters, of which they had already seen quite enough to satisfy any morbid curiosity they might have felt.

"Here," whispered the prince, although he could almost have shouted without fear of being overheard above the general uproar, "we must awaken Miss Weston."

Jones saw his dark form bending over at the foot of the slender tree, and knew that he had laid his burden down.

"Shall I light up?" inquired Jones in an equally low tone, and speaking close to his companion's ear.

"On no account. Not yet, that is. Will you hold up her head, please? That is right. Now—this liquor would well-nigh rouse life in the dusty veins of an Egyptian mummy."

"If it's the same you gave me, you're right. Look out—there's something behind you—look out, I say!"

Over Sergius' shoulder he had caught a glimpse of two green eyes glaring, balls of fire set in the black velvet of night. Sergius, with the swiftness of a prestidigitateur, replaced the stopper in the small flask he had been holding to Miss Weston's lips, reached with unerring grasp for one of the rifles laid across Jones' lap, rose from knees to feet in the same motion and laughed softly and lowered the weapon. Stooping, he picked up a small stone and flung it straight at the glaring eyes. There was a startled snarl, a fiendish yell, and the eyes vanished, accompanied by a scuffling and crashing in the underbrush.

"A hyena," commented Sergius, resuming his interrupted task with unruffled composure. "No use wasting a shot on that sort of vermin."

"Good Heavens, man, have you the eyes of a cat? How could you tell what it was?"

"Oh, I can see better than most in the dark, I will admit. I should never have suggested this venture if it were not so. Now—ah, she is awakening."

There was a cough, a little, strangled gasp, and Miss Weston sat up very suddenly. Unlike more ordinary people, she did not exclaim "Where am I?" although the query would certainly have been excusable, but seemed to spring instantly to full consciousness and knowledge of the situation.

Without a moment's hesitation she reached up in the darkness and delivered a slap in Sergius' general direction which would have been splendidly effective had he not sprung back with the same speed he had shown in dealing with the hyena. A second later she was on her feet, panting and sobbing, but not, Jones feared, with panic.

"Oh, you did it—you did it! You cowards! You left them there and carried me away when I was helpless. Oh—if I live till morning you shall be punished for this. You shall, I say!"

Gently, but with irresistible strength, Sergius took her small hands in one of his, and placed the other over her mouth.

"Be silent," he said softly and sternly. "You must not endanger your own life because of your anger against me. Paul and the rest are, a thousand times more secure at this moment than we, unless you control yourself and use your splendid vigor and determination to a better purpose than recrimination. If I release my hold, will you come with us quietly and softly?"

A miracle occurred, for Miss Weston yielded—on that one point, at least. She must have nodded her head, although Jones could not see the motion in the darkness, for Sergius released her and stepped back.

"Do not imagine that you have greater concern for my brother than I, Miss Weston. We placed them all in safety, barricaded the entrance, and built a fire which will burn until morning. And now, you will please keep between Mr. Jones and myself. If we run, you must run also; and if we should crouch suddenly down, you must do likewise. Do you understand?"

"I understand," came the answer in a tone of suppressed rebellion.

"Very well. Will you give me one of those torches, Roland? You have your rifle ready and cocked?"

"Yes—but I'm a darned bad shot."

The nihilist sighed. "One cannot expect everything," he said. "If I tell you to shoot, aim between the eyes—you are likely to see them; at any rate. And now, forward!"

Two long, white beams sprang into being, and by the shifting rays Mr. Jones saw the narrow, trodden trail from which they had emerged in the afternoon. More than ever he marveled at Sergius' almost supernatural abilities. How had he managed to strike that one single place where they had a bare chance of entering the jungle successfully?

The Russian led the way, followed by Miss Weston, and Jones brought up the rear. And now they had entered the very center of pandemonium itself. Roars, shrieks, grunts, bellows rent the air upon every side.

"Don't be frightened!" Sergius called back over his shoulder. "These torches will keep most of the brutes off—but, good God, not this one!"

Jones caught, a glimpse of a mighty bulk rearing itself high over the head of their leader; there were three sharp, rapid reports; then the thing, whatever it was, with a terrific snarl of rage, had lurched forward and downward upon the unfortunate nihilist. Miss Weston, with remarkable presence of mind, had turned, run back to Jones's side, and then turned again to face this midnight terror, without a scream or act which could have impeded her sole remaining guardian.

He, staring with horror down his little, wavering beam of light, saw only a monstrous black head with snarling, savage jaws and two red eyes that glared like coals of fire.

"Shoot him—shoot him!" It was Miss Weston's voice, and she was shaking his arm viciously. "Shoot him—or give me that rifle!"

"Between the eyes!" gasped Jones.

"You're likely to see them!"

He had no idea of what he was saying, or that he had spoken. Then, as he stood there, shaking in every limb, he suddenly reached the extremity of terror, and passed beyond it into that unnatural coolness and calm which is so efficient and, sometimes, so hard to reach. The trembling palsy passed, and every nerve and muscle tautened to abnormal firmness. From numbed quiescence his brain leaped to lightning action.

He knew what he, "a darned bad shot," must do if he would save the friend who lay invisible somewhere under that dreadful head.

With a sure swiftness of which none of his acquaintances would have deemed Jones capable, he handed the electric torch to the girl, darted forward to within ten feet of the monster, raised his rifle and fired, aiming at the center of the forehead, and pumping one cartridge after another into place as fast as he could work the lever.

Undoubtedly the fact that the brute had paused at all in its attack was due to the dazzling effect of the electric torch, and if it had not been for an unusual piece of luck Jones would probably never have lived to marvel at his own feat. For at the first report the light-blinded brute snarled again, started to lift itself, failed, drooped, and sank slowly down upon the path. Jones, however, emptied his magazine before he realized that he had actually killed the creature with that first fortunate bullet.

Then he called back to the girl: "Come quick, Miss Weston; we've got to pull it off from Sergius!"

She ran up, still bearing the light, and the two looked down in consternation at the mighty bulk which lay like a monstrous black tombstone over the body of Sergius Petrofsky. It was a great, hairless mountain of flesh, The dropped head looked like the face of some gargoyle carven in unpolished ebony. Its fore legs were invisible, doubled under the body. Move it? They might as well have tried to move an elephant.

Nevertheless, catching hold of the upstanding, rounded ears, they tugged and heaved with all their might, but could only succeed in shifting the head a little to one side.

"Sergius! Sergius!" cried Miss Weston, dropping suddenly in a little heap of pathos beside that mountain of brute flesh.

She was answered by a moan. To their amazement, it did not come from beneath the monster, but from some little distance to one side of the path. Yet it was certainly a human moan, for it was followed by a voice: "Over here. I'm—I'm coming."

Miss Weston sprang to her feet and accompanied Jones in a wild rush toward the voice. There, sprawled out among the flowering, tangled vines, they found the nihilist himself; and as the circle of light struck his face, he sat and stared back at them with an amazement equal to their own.

"What—what hit me?" he gasped.

Jones laughed aloud in his relief. "It did. How in the name of all the saints did you get here?"

Sergius passed a bewildered hand over his head. "I—I begin to remember. Something seemed to come right up out of the ground. I—I fired at it—and then—and then—"

"It must have struck you with its paw and knocked you clear away from the path," interrupted Miss Weston in a calm, indifferent voice. Jones glanced at her in astonishment. Was this the girl who had been sobbing out the name of Sergius a few minutes before? "If you are hurt, you had better get up and go on with us—although I would suggest that you let Mr. Jones take the lead, as he seems much the better shot."

Jones helped his friend to rise, and as he did so Sergius laughed without a trace of annoyance. "If you actually killed that brute, my friend, Miss Weston is right. Did you kill it?"

"I must have, because it's certainly dead, although I can hardly believe it myself. What on earth is the thing, Sergius?"

They had recovered the narrow path and stood beside the black hulk which blocked it entirely, overlapping on both sides into the underbrush.

Sergius examined the huge head with interest. "I never saw anything exactly like it before. Where did you hit it?"

"Between the eyes. You remember you told me to fire between the eyes, so I did. I fired about ten cartridges into it, but I think it died at the first shot."

The nihilist looked up at him with a curious expression. "It did? That's rather odd. The beast has a frontal bone as thick as a rhinoceros', if I am any judge. No; here are three bullets embedded in the bone, but not a sign of a hole. Ah, that was it, eh? My friend, by very well-deserved good luck your first bullet did not strike the forehead at all, but penetrated this left eye and went straight into the brain."

"Great Scot!" exclaimed the American. "And I was about ten feet away! It's a good thing the brute has a head as big as a barn-door, or I'd have missed it entirely."

Sergius smiled. "Nevertheless, you deserve great congratulations. If your first bullet had not gone a few inches astray, we should perhaps none of us be alive at this moment. But what a strange brute it is! I should say it was a monstrous bear, from the shape of the head, if it were not so hairless. I wonder, now, if this is the creature that pulled up the death cabbages there by the plane?"

"Prince Sergius," again interrupted Miss Weston, with a slightly impatient note in her voice, "would it not be better to come back in daylight to continue your zoological researches? If this creature has a mate, and it should come this way, Mr. Jones might not be able to kill the second one."

"And you are quite sure, after what has happened, that as a protector I am an entire failure, eh? Well, perhaps you are justified, but still I had better continue to lead the way. What do you think, Roland Jones?"

"Don't be absurd. I'm a rank, bungling amateur, and you both know it. Shall we climb over this thing, or go around it?"

"The underbrush is thick here—and there might be snakes, though we have seen none. I think we had better use your victim as a causeway."

The two men helped Miss Weston up to the gigantic shoulders, and they walked the length of the huge creature, more and more amazed at its bulk. From nose to hind quarters it must have measured a full fifteen feet, and in his heart Jones wished that he might have transported the head to his rooms in New York. How he could have gloated over the surprise of a friend of his who was a big game-hunter and very proud of certain rhino-heads and lion-skins, trophies of African expeditions.

He reloaded his rifle carefully and resumed his position as rear-guard with a new confidence in its powers which took no heed to the fact that only by a lucky accident had his shot struck a vulnerable spot.

Many times as they marched silently ahead, the underbrush by the wayside swayed and bent, crackling, to the passage of animals of which they caught not even a glimpse. Once a lynxlike beast as big as a large panther dropped silently into the middle of the path ahead of them, glared for a second into the bull's-eye of Sergius, and with another spring was gone before he could fire at it.

This incident, however, encouraged the three, for it seemed as if most of the jungle inhabitants shunned the blinding electric lights as they would have shunned a campfires.

And at length there came to their nostrils a whiff of noxious odor which told the two men that they had successfully passed the first barriers to their escape. Vile smell though it was, it came welcome enough just then, for it was the odor of the fungi that grew about the roots of the death cabbages.

Jones realized with pleasure that they had passed the great spider's trap without even being aware of it. He had subconsciously dreaded more than anything also going past that dark incline, at the foot of which waited the thing of long, black, shining legs and protuberant eyes.

But as the full force of the stench enveloped them, Miss Weston stopped dead, so that Jones almost collided with her in the narrow path.

"Stop—I can't go on into this—this horrible vapor!" she called after Sergius. He heard, for he turned back immediately and returned to where they stood.

"What is the matter?" he asked a trifle impatiently.

"This dreadful smell. I can't—"

"Miss Weston, a smell won't kill anybody. At least, this one will not. Mr. Jones and myself were in the midst of it for nearly an hour, and we were not harmed."

"But—"

"Do you wish to be left here, then?"

The question was brutal, but it served its purpose. A moment the girl was silent; then she threw back her shoulders and smiled contemptuously. "I presume you would not hesitate to do that, either. No, I will not oblige you by relieving you of my hampering company. I can certainly face anything that you can."

Sergius looked at her with plain admiration on his face.

"Believe me, Miss Weston, this charnel odor is no worse than that of the battle-fields to which you were going. I have been there, also. Will you take my arm now? For we must walk through a very disagreeable place."

"No, thank you!" she—well, she snapped, although it isn't a nice thing to say of a heroine. "I am sure Mr. Jones will offer all the help I may need."

"Very well." The prince shrugged, and without more ado they passed from the forest of slender palms into the safe way, broken, perhaps, by the very creature which they had encountered and ungratefully slain that night.

CHAPTER XI

As the three staggered out, one after another, from the acid-fumed fungi onto the wiry grass of the central space, their ears were rent by a sound of hideous and continued screaming which drowned out all other noise entirely. Startled and shuddering, both Sergius and Jones directed the rays of their lanterns toward the sound, and a most extraordinary picture leaped into view.

The scene of the tragedy was one of the larger death-cabbages. Its seventyfive-foot leaves were spread almost flat, and all the inner tentacles were writhing and squirming upward, so that at first glance it looked as if this vegetable flesh-eater were all on fire with slim, scarlet flames. Then, as they moved their search-lights upward, they saw what it was that screamed.

Clinging with huge claws to the upper stalk, just below the tuft, was a dark, winged thing, and all about its body and head the tentacles were wound and fastened. So wide were its frantically beating wings that even where they stood, a hundred yards away, the wind of them struck their faces in heavy gusts. The stalk swayed and bent under the strain, but the tentacles had firm hold, and continually new scarlet cords shot upward to aid in the binding of the captive, until its body was no more than a bundle of flaming red.

The screaming grew weaker; the wings fluttered spasmodically for a few moments longer, then drooped down helpless. The tentacles took hold upon them, also. Into the field of light a pointed, serrated thing rose slowly, followed by others upon all sides. The death cabbage was closing its doors to feast in sacred privacy.

A moment later the vision of trapped prey was shut from their eyes.

With a long, shuddering sigh, Sergius turned his own light slowly about the grim ranks encircling the glade. Everywhere it fell upon spread leaves and living, ready tentacles Only one or two other of the cabbages were closed. Doubtless their dinner had come to them earlier in the evening.

"What are they? What is this place you have brought me to?"

It was Miss Weston. Both men turned to her with a guilty start, realizing that in their fascinated absorption they had for the time forgotten her.

"I am so sorry," apologized Sergius, as if he and Jones had invented the vegetable horrors, as her tone implied.

"It is like—it is like a circle from Dante's Inferno!" exclaimed Jones, laying his hand pityingly on the girl's arm, and wishing with all his heart that he had never acceded to Sergius' wishes; that they had left the girl at the caves, or stayed there themselves. What might not the effect of having witnessed such a scene be upon the mind of a delicate, high-strung woman?

But she drew slightly away, and spoke again to the Russian. From first to last she gave Mr. Jones no more attention than one grants to a supernumerary—a necessary adjunct to the play, but scarcely of more human interest than the furniture.

"You are sorry!" she repeated scornfully. "Your sorrow is rather late, it appears. Where is the aeroplane?"

The nihilist bowed gallantly to her contemptuous tone.

"As usual, Miss Weston, you speak directly to the point. The aeroplane is—why, where in the name of Heaven is it?"

For his light, flashing up the glade, encountered only empty space. The aeroplane, which they had left not far from where they now stood, had disappeared.

Jones felt his heart begin a slow, systematic descent toward his toes. If the machine were actually gone, what would they do? Then he gave a joyful cry as his own light, dancing spritelike over the grass, flashed upon something broad-winged and motionless over near the wilted death-cabbage which had so nearly made a meal of him and Sergius.

"There it is! It's all right! It's there!"

"Thank God!" breathed Miss Weston, frightened momentarily out of her attitude of disdainful indifference.

"But how did it get there?" frowned Sergius. "Miss Weston, you must not go so near as that to the cabbagges. Will you wait here with Mr. Jones, while I go after the plane?"

"I will not," she replied instantly. "We will either all go, or none of us will go, whichever you please. Oh, I'm not troubled for your safety, Prince Sergius. Don't imagine that. But if you should be killed or injured, who is to pilot the plane?

"I am overwhelmed by your solicitude for me," murmured Sergius, bowing again. "If you must go, keep behind us. Here, take this light and one of the rifles. Yes, please, I want my hands free. Come on, then."

He set off at a swinging stride, followed by Jones and Miss Weston, who looked pale by the reflected light of her lantern, but very determined indeed.

The plane, they found, was fairly in the midst of the many-colored fungi. But worse, and more important, it was quite near to a thirty-foot vegetable which they had just had good testimony, would make no more than a good meal on all three of them. In fact, as they approached, it seemed to sense them, and stretched out a dozen hungry tentacles in their direction. Two or three of these, feeling blindly, encountered a rear strut of the aeroplane and curled about it. Then the tentacles contracted suddenly, and the aeroplane rolled backward an inch or so.

"That won't do," cried the nihilist, and seizing a forward strut he braced himself and pulled, but with no apparent effect. More tentacles reached toward him as he stood there, but he was partly shielded from them by the plane itself.

To his credit be it said that Mr. Jones, without an instant's hesitation, dropped his rifle, handed his torch to Miss Weston, and springing to Sergius' side flung his weight also into the tug-of-war. But it was evident that the strength of the vegetable was greater than their combined efforts. The utmost they could, do was to hold the machine where it was.

After several muscle and nerve-straining minutes, the nihilist said to Jones in a low voice, not to be overheard by the girl, "My friend, there is only one thing to be done and that is creep back there, over the tail, and cut some of those tentacles."

"Impossible! Why, the others would get you in a second."

"I don't care if they do. I will cut them also. They are strong, but a knife goes through them easily. Do you not remember yesterday afternoon? Miss Weston, will you keep both lights trained on the rear of the plane for a few moments, please? I am going to try something."

"I won't let you do it—" began Jones, but with a spring Sergius had mounted upon the plane and was working his way toward the rear.

The withdrawal of his strength was accompanied by a surge of the aeroplane backward, and Jones had to use all his muscle and attention to keep it in place. Sergius was now out of his sight, but by a sudden swaying and jolting and a scream from Margaret Weston, he knew that his too-daring companion must have been found by one or more of the questing tentacles.

The machine swayed again violently, then he heard Sergius' voice.

"Hold those lights steady, Miss Weston. Ah! two at once. Roland, we needn't have been so worried— one might as well be afraid of a stick of celery. You devil! Would you?"

There was a strangled, gasping sound, another scream from the girl, then the Russian's voice again, somewhat hoarser but still cheerful. "He almost got me that time—but not twice! That is right. Send me a few more feelers! Pull! Pull, Jones, with all your force!"

Jones obeyed with the strength of desperation, as a sudden lightening in the weight and a renewed swaying told him that Sergius had jumped to the ground, Slowly at first, then with gathering ease and speed the plane moved. In a minute it was out of the fungi and rolling clear upon the turf.

The second that he dared, Jones let go and ran around to the rear. To his great relief there was his nihilist friend, leaning against, a strut and wiping his forehead. Miss Weston joined them with the lights, and they all stared at one another in silence.

Then Sergius dropped his handkerchief, and brought his hand down upon his thigh with a resounding slap.

"What a fool I am!" he exclaimed. "What an utter fool! All I had to do was to climb into the pilot's seat and start the propeller. Even that brute could hardly have outpulled the engine. And my neck would have been saved a very unpleasant experience." He felt of it tenderly, then laughed.

"Well, it is over now. Some inquisitive beast must have come by here and given the plane a push, so that it rolled down that little incline."

He began a careful examination of wires, struts, taut varnished canvas, propeller blades and last, and most important, the engine itself and its tank. In a few minutes now their very lives might depend upon the thoroughness of that examination.

"I can find nothing wrong," he said at last, and his announcement was greeted with an involuntary sigh of relief from both his companions.

"Miss Weston," he continued, "I think you and Mr. Jones can manage to occupy that seat together. At any rate, in a few minutes we will be out of this intolerable odor. Here, Miss Weston, put on my coat, since you will find it cold in the upper air, if you will be so kind as to cover your face with your hands when we get up, you will not need goggles. Are we all ready?"

"I shall certainly not take your coat," said the girl indignantly, waving the garment away. "Not that your comfort is so important, but I know a little about flying, and if you became numbed by the cold, what would happen to us?"

Sergius laughed. "There is no danger of my becoming numbed in the few minutes that we will be in the air. Your dress is a great deal thinner than my tunic. I am sorry, but you will have to take it or we cannot start."

"Let her take mine," interposed Jones. "I have nothing to do but sit still, and it really doesn't matter whether I get numb or not.

"You are very kind, Mr. Jones." Miss Weston smiled sweetly upon him. "Yes, since you insist, I shall be glad to borrow your coat."

And suiting the action to the words she took it from him and slipped into it. Sergius frowned and looked as if he were about to say something, then checked himself and turned away, putting on his own coat without any further protest. But Mr. Jones caught what looked like an expression of amused triumph on Margaret Weston's beautiful face. It was the first time that she had really succeeded in annoying Sergius Petrofsky.

A few minutes later, having pushed the machine to the extreme end of the glade, turned so as to face the open run, they all took their places and strapped themselves in. The rear seat was a tight fit indeed for both Jones and Miss Weston, but it was only to be for a few minutes, and the girl murmured that at least she was glad she did not have to sit so close to Sergius.

Mr. Jones might have felt more flattered if she had not put in the "at least."

The Russian started his engine, the propeller began to revolve, and a second later the plane rolled forward across the uneven grass. They did not gather speed very quickly, however, and it looked as if the machine would refuse to rise in the limited course. Twice Sergius raised the elevator, and twice the plane continued on its rough and bouncing course up the glade, refusing to leave the earth.

They were now perilously close to the further end and the plane was running at a speed of about sixty miles an hour. To stop was impossible, and for a time it seemed as if their career was to end in the maw of a particularly wide-spread and hungry-looking death-cabbage, when just at the last minute he again raised the elevator, the plane tilted slightly and took the air beneath its taut canvas wings.

They barely cleared the crest of the deadly vegetable, and with their hearts still in their throats found themselves shooting onward and upward, away from the valley of death.

Yet even as they drew in their first full breaths of relief and clean, cool air, Death itself, though in another form, rose after them.

The first consciousness that they were the object of attack came as Sergius banked his wings and swung in a wide circle, preparatory to straightening out on the seaward course. As the machine tilted against the light breeze, a large, dark thing shot by its nose, just missing the plane by a foot or so, and causing even the iron-nerved Russian momentarily to lose control.

The plane dipped and shot downward at a dangerous angle. They had risen scarcely four hundred feet, and there was not much room for evolutions. He just saved them from destruction, and rose again, casting anxious glances about in the darkness, for they had extinguished the electric torches before rising.

The girl was not aware that anything had happened, for she had covered her face with her hands to shield it from the sharp wind of their flight. Jones stared about as anxiously as their pilot, but could see nothing. Sergius' eyes must have been, as he had said, of an unusual kind, for presently he shouted and pointed into the darkness.

A second later something huge came up from below, actually grazed the left wing, and was gone again.

Jones knew that the dark thing must be one of the flying monsters, of which this was the third they had encountered, and he earnestly hoped that its interference was purely accidental. He said nothing, fearing to frighten Miss Weston, but on a sudden impulse he loosened the strap that held bah of them, with a vague idea that if they should be flung to the earth they might have some chance of jumping clear.

That Sergius was fully aware of the danger was made evident, for he began to climb in a swift, steep spiral. Birds of the night hardly ever fly high, and if they could reach the upper levels of the air, so easily accessible to them, they would be safe.

But the evil genius of Joker Island had no idea of permitting them to escape so simply. Again, with a wild beating of vast pinions, the winged peril was upon them. This time it struck downward from above and even the skill of the nihilist could not save them.

Of what happened next Mr. Jones was never able to give a coherent account. Probably the weight and impact of the creature partially stunned him. At any rate, his next conscious memory was of finding himself swinging and dangling over empty space, his arms and hands firmly buried in something that felt like warm fur, and that he was being carried along in great swoops and lunges, so that it required his utmost strength to keep from being jerked off.

CHAPTER XII

Wide, frantic wings were beating on either side of him, and even in that desperate moment he realized that he must have grasped the flying monster at the instant it struck the aeroplane. Doubtless much against its will, it was now carrying him along as an equally unwilling passenger.

As a matter of fact, he was clinging to its fur and the skin of its breast, which was fortunately very loose, affording an excellent handhold. But Mr. Jones was no acrobat, although he was certainly playing the part of one. Already his hands were numb and aching. He wondered if he could manage to climb around and up to the creature's back, but gave it up as a feat too great for his weakening muscles.

Suddenly he found himself laughing wildly. He had remembered the story of Sindbad and the Roc, which had carried him into the Valley of Diamonds. But the Roc bore the sailor in its claws, and this creature was not half so obliging.

Looking downward, Jones was sure that they were far higher than when the beast had struck them. He should, even swinging so dizzily through the air, have caught a glimpse of light where the fire must still be blazing by the cliff, or perhaps, if they were very high, the lights of the other encampment outside the wall. But all beneath was a black void, under what seemed a swirling, dancing firmament of stars.

Then, sick and giddy, the moment came when Jones knew he must shortly let go his grip upon skin and fur and whirl down, breathless, helpless, into the waiting arms of death. Suddenly he began to kick violently, and swing his body from side to side. If he went he was determined that his involuntary captor should go with him.

Came a harsh scream from above, a few mad circles, and then, though the wings still beat, he knew that they were dropping with dangerous speed through the empty blackness of space.

The fall, however, ended a great deal sooner than Jones anticipated, and not upon the earth but in the sea. There was one terrific splash, as beast and man struck the water.

Mr. Jones, being of course underneath, had decidedly the worst of the dive. In the first place he had expected to be hurled into the maw of a death-cabbage, perhaps, or to be dashed to pieces upon the earth, or, if he were lucky, that they might break their fall upon the crest of one of the tall, slender palms. The one thing which he did not anticipate was to be plunged into a cold bath. His mouth was open, and his lungs nearly empty of air when it happened, and the consequence was that he nearly drowned before recovered sufficient sense to let go of the fur to which he was still clinging with the tenacity of the dying.

Even then it was more by good luck than presence of mind that he reached the surface, for all the water was in a whirl with the flapping struggles of the creature which had brought him there. Fortunately, although evidently it could not swim, its convulsive efforts pushed it along, so that Jones came up at last a few feet clear of the worst of the turmoil.

The sea was running in long, smooth, oily swells, nearly as kind as quiet water to the gasping swimmer. He cleared his lungs, then turned on his back and floated, drawing in the air in huge draughts.

As his blood became re-oxygenated, he began to feel a certain curiosity. What had become of the enemy? Turning again he swam slowly and quietly, reserving his strength, and looking anxiously about from the top of each swell as it came under him.

The sea, which was free that night from the phosphorescence that often characterizes those waters, reflected very little light, from the stars. He could see nothing—no land, no monster—nothing but the stars above and beneath—blackness. He felt as if he had been dropped into a sea of India ink, a sea where no man or beast had ever come or sun shone upon.

Then he remembered the possibility of sharks and hoped devoutly that no company of that sort would arrive.

His clothes dragged him down, and he determined to be rid of them, at least. He kicked off his shoes and at last, by working carefully, got rid of his khaki tunic. The puttees were hardest to deal with, but he finally got them off, followed them with his breeches, and even shed the thin, loose-fitting silk underwear, as a last slight impediment to what he intended to be a fight to the finish for life and the chance to get back and finish his voluntary job of helping Sergius, or find and bury his remains. The latter contingency seemed the more likely one.

The water was warm, the slow, even swells friendly, and Mr. Jones felt sure that he could keep afloat till dawn, which could not now be far off. What he would do then depended upon circumstances, but he did not really believe the flying monster could have carried him far out to sea, and he hoped that when day broke he would see Joker Island within easy swimming distance. Until then it would be dangerous to strike out, perhaps in the wrong direction, so he floated a great deal, only swimming enough to keep his blood in circulation.

In one of the periods when he was on his back, his ears in consequence being under water, there reached them a peculiar, vibratory, explosive sound. He had heard it before, while floating in the quiet reaches of Long Island Sound, and with a great rush of hope Jones turned over and trod water raising himself as far as he could above the surface and staring from right to left through the blind veil of night.

Nothing.

He turned himself slowly, waiting for the rise of each successive swell to look long. Then he gave a wild shout and letting himself drop back struck out with frantic strokes.

Very small, very far away, he had seen two lights which were not stars, for one was red and one was green.

Had his mood of exultation lasted long he must have perished even on the threshold of salvation, for such a pace as he had set himself would have exhausted the most expert swimmer. Fortunately common sense returned in time, and he realized that since he saw both the red and the green it must mean but one thing. The vessel, whatever it was, was approaching him, probably at a far greater speed than he could possibly attain even if he could have kept it up.

He "loafed" again, rising on each swell with the deadly fear that this time one of the lights would have disappeared, sinking again into the trough with the blissful assurance that both lights still shone.

There is nothing much harder than to estimate distance at night across water. Knowing this from his own yachting experience, Jones floated several times, listening for the engine beat which the sea carried so much farther than the wind. And each time he fancied that it was louder, more distinct.

At last he raised himself again upon the crest of a swell and sent a long, anxious hail across the waste. To his inexpressible joy it was immediately answered.

Ten minutes later Mr. Roland C. Jones was picked up out of the watery vastness of the Pacific Ocean by his own power cruiser, the Bandersnatch, which had for three days been cross-quartering those waters in the vain, despairing hope of picking up some trace of him or his body.

CHAPTER XIII

Although the fact was not included in the extensive notices which later appeared in the New York papers in regard to the loss and rescue of the well-known millionaire yachtsman (his own friends told nothing, but one of the sailors talked), there occurred a peculiar psychological phenomenon as Mr. Jones came over the rail of the Bandersnatch.

It was as if a dark veil, which he had scarcely known existed, had been suddenly swept away from his mental vision. It had torn a trifle when he recognized one of the men in the dingey which rescued him as his old friend, Henry Martindale. He had sat in a silent, stupid-seeming daze as they were rowed back to the yacht by the sailor who accompanied Martindale, and listened to his friends' exclamations of joy, amazement and congratulation.

But as he stepped, barefooted and naked, upon the white deck of his own, familiar, beloved Bandersnatch, that veil split asunder from top to bottom and vanished forever from his brain.

In plain words, Mr. Jones remembered. He remembered how for two years, since the moment when a small, heavy clock, carelessly placed upon a shelf in his stateroom on the Lusitania, had fallen at a lurch of the vessel and struck him upon the temple, he had been the victim of that queer mental disease, amnesia. Cared for by the best doctors in London and New York, they had not been able to restore the delicate equilibrium of his brain.

The loss of his memory had been accompanied by physical deterioration, and this winter the physicians had ordered a long cruise through Southern seas in the hope of improving, if not curing, his condition.

They had, exactly as he had informed Jim Haskins, come around into the Pacific by way of the Panama Canal, and were bound for the Philippines when one night Mr. Jones actually did get up out of bed, dress himself, not in yachting clothes but in a grey morning suit, walk out on deck, straight across it, and over the rail, before the men on watch could stop him. In the sea that was running they had been unable to find him, but, although they had from almost the first, given him up as drowned, still his good friends Martindale and Charles Laroux could not bear to leave the spot of the disaster, but cruised up and down, back and forth, for three whole days and nights, ever on the lookout, ever hoping against hope that they might at least bear his body back to New York for burial.

Upon falling overboard the shock of his sudden immersion in the sea had, by one of those little jokes which Nature sometimes perpetrates, started his mental machinery going again at exactly the place where, figuratively, it left the rails. The equal shock of finding his rescuers to be his friends, and the rescuing vessel the Bandersnatch, completed the good work, and that deep abyss of two forgotten years, wherein had been lost the great war and many other memories less vast, was filled.

Once again he could spread out before him the pages of his past life and find not one leaf missing.

Curiously enough, his first thought, after the sweeping realization of it all came over him, was of his cousin, the Hon. Percy Merridale, whom he had been going to visit on that unlucky voyage across the Atlantic.

"Poor old Percy," he said, paying no heed to the flood of questions which were pouring from the lips of both his friends, "why, he was killed along with half his regiment at the very beginning of the war. And here I have been wondering what he would think because I did not arrive in London on time!"

"You have, eh?" asked Laroux, looking at him keenly. "Then you remember that you did start for London?"

"Oh, yes. I remember everything now. Lord, what chums you fellows have been, putting up with the crazy whims of a man with only half a mind. But by Jove, I'm cold. If you'll have the steward get me something hot to drink, and let me get dry and into some clothes, I'll be glad to tell you all about it."

With bitter self-reproaches at their own neglectfulness, Laroux and Martindale fairly hustled him below and to bed. They would hear nothing of his dressing, but on one thing he held out. He was perfectly willing to go to sleep—he had never felt so utterly tired out in his life—but they must promise to hold the Bandersnatch where she was, or at least near to it, until he awakened.

To this his friends agreed, and Jones slept the sleep of exhausted but perfect health for eleven straight hours.

It was three o'clock in the afternoon when he appeared on deck, and he immediately sought his two friends. They greeted him eagerly, for they were more than anxious to know how he could possibly have kept afloat for nearly three days, and settling comfortably down beneath the awnings on the breezy afterdeck, they all lighted their excellent cigars and the story began.

Before he had progressed very far their interest became other than that of curiosity, and as he went on, two of the three cigars were allowed to languish and die unheeded. From curiosity they passed to amazement, and from amazement to carefully suppressed incredulity.

This, however, caused Jones no uneasiness, for it was about what he had expected. Finishing the incident of the flying monster with the utmost complacence and indifference to their more than dubious glances, he called for Captain Janiver.

"Captain," he said, "I want you to locate for me an island which I know to be in this immediate vicinity, although beyond the horizon in some direction. What land is there hereabouts?"

The captain shook his head. "The only island I know of within a hundred miles is hardly worthy of the name, Mr. Jones. It is nothing but a high, barren chunk of rock sticking up out of the sea. As far as I know it has never even been named."

"Oh, yes, it has," smiled Jones. "That island is Joker Island, and I want you to put the old Bandersnatch's nose about and take us there just as fast as she'll slouch through the water."

"Very well, sir, but—"

"Why, Jones, old man, we were at that place ourselves, and there isn't anything there!" This from Laroux.

"You were there?"

"Of course. Janiver remembered the place and we went, on the slim possibility that you might have been washed ashore. We cruised all around it, and even landed wherever there was a beach. We found some footprints and a few old, tin cans, but there was certainly nothing else."

Jones grew suddenly very white. He had a sensation of sickness in the pit of his stomach, and an overwhelming consciousness of some dreadful disaster impending, he himself scarcely knew what.

"Captain Janiver," he said between his teeth, "put this boat about and do as I directed."

The captain touched his cap and obeyed, not without a curious glance over his shoulder. He was familiar with the idiosyncrasies of his owner—all developed, however, within the past twenty-four months, and he sighed as he gave the necessary directions.

"Too bad," he murmured, shaking his gray head sadly, "too bad. Such a good-natured, quiet young fellow as he is, too."

As for Jones himself, he resolutely declined to speak another word on the subject until he had himself visited the scene of his recent adventures. Clinging passionately to the belief that they had actually occurred, he forced his mind to dwell upon the question of what might have happened to Sergius and Miss Weston after he left the aeroplane in such an unexpected manner.

He was possessed by a really loving concern upon this matter, although the love was not for the Boston girl but for Sergius Petrofsky, who had in the short space of three days won a place in his heart never before occupied by any man, even his faithful friends Harry Martindale and Charlie Laroux.

The two latter let him alone, when they perceived that he no longer wished to talk. Like the captain, they, were accustomed to some rather strange moods in their friend, although they had hoped for better things with the recovery of his memory.

About five o'clock the rapid little Bandersnatch raised a blur upon the southern horizon, which soon developed into a dark blot, then gradually took shape as the familiar black outline of the crater-wall of Joker Island.

With the sight all Jones's courage returned. He could not sit still, but paced back and forth across the deck, and when at last they came to; anchor in the very bay where the Monterey had lain, he fairly tumbled into the small launch which was lowered to accommodate Jones, his two friends and a couple of sailors.

Of course the Monterey was gone, but there was the place where the nihilists had been encamped, though now no tents raised their brown canvas against the cliff, Springing from the launch Jones rushed up the beach and examined the place where they had been. There were, as Laroux had said, a few tin cans scattered about, a good many footprints, and the ashes of a fire, but these might have been there for any length of time.

He ran down the beach, hoping to discover the marks left by the aeroplane's launching, but this had been upon the smooth, hard sand near the water, and the tides had obliterated them, if they had really ever been there. If they had been there! But they had been—it had happened! It was all so indelibly imprinted upon the tablets of his brain that it was clearer than any other event in his whole life.

The caves, then. Beckoning to Laroux and Martindale to follow him, he pressed on to the rocky promontory hiding the cleft, or ravine. Well, that was there anyway. And there were caves, too, hundreds of them. Into which of them had he crawled, following Prince Paul and Miss Weston, followed by Jim Haskins and the two sailors? This one surely, or—no, it might have been this, or any one of a dozen others.

He felt the touch of a hand upon his shoulder.

"Look here, old man," said Martindale with a gentle indulgence which seemed to Jones well-nigh intolerable by reason of its implications, "you must not take this so hard. Now listen. Charlie and I know you are absolutely all right now—absolutely all right. Don't let there be any question in your mind of that. Your memory has returned, and you can go on to the Philippines, or back to New York and take up your life exactly where you were before it—that accident on the liner—happened.

"But just now you are suffering from the memory of a particularly vivid hallucination. If we didn't think you were all O.K. we wouldn't tell you that, you know. We'd humor you, and say we thought it was all real. But you wouldn't want us to do that now, would you? You'll believe, won't you, that while you were here on the beach, thrown-up by the storm you—well, dreamed a whole lot of things that couldn't possibly have happened? Then, still dreaming, you started to swim out to sea again, thinking you were pursued by these impossible monsters, and so we picked you up, by about one chance in a million. The currents are very strong about here, Janiver says, and they carried you a long way—clear out of sight of the island. Can't you believe all this, which is the truth, and let the rest go along with the last two years?"

He spoke earnestly, with a deep and loving tenderness, which made Jones extremely uncomfortable. How could he convince these men that those things had really happened? That there, within the island, was at least one other friend of his, possibly in dire need of help, if he yet lived? Then Holloway, Prince Paul, Haskins, the beautiful, sharp-tongued girl-

Suddenly the mental defenses which he had raised gave way and went down before the flood of damning, almost unendurable conviction.

"Harry," he said hoarsely, staggering a little where he stood, "will you and Laroux get me back to New York? Just put up with me till—till we get back to New York, won't you?"

"Don't be a fool, Rolly," cried Laroux, springing forward and actually shaking him, but with a roughness that was all friendship. "You aren't crazy—you never have been crazy—you've been in a sort of delirium, like you have when you're down with fever. You're right as Harry or me. If you weren't you wouldn't be ready to believe the truth. It was nothing but plain, ordinary delirium, I tell you."

"Well, maybe it was," conceded Jones, with a somewhat sickly smile, "but whatever it was, I know I want to get away from this place and back to New York. I want to see brick buildings, and ride on every-day street-cars, and eat dinner in a Broadway cafe. You boys have been the best, most patient friends a man ever had. Will you promise me something?"

"Of course," broke in Laroux, "but look here, Rolly, just to satisfy you entirely suppose we stop in at Frisco and find out if such a yacht as the Monterey was chartered recently by a bunch of Russians, and—"

Jones held up his hand. "No," he said. "A man who's been off his nut for two years, and knows it, doesn't have to go around hunting up evidence to support the facts. I want to get back to New York just as fast as the old tub will travel. What I want you to promise is this. Don't ever mention any of this—this crazy dream of mine to me again. I know you won't tell it to anybody else. But—I just don't want ever to hear anything about it—again."

CHAPTER XIV

Three months had elapsed, and Mr. Roland C. Jones remained, to all appearances, a well and mentally sound man. Back in New York he quietly resumed the peaceful pursuits of his easy-going, pleasant, bachelor life. Laroux and Martindale adhered strictly and honorably to their promise and never mentioned to any one the singular delusion which had marked the termination of their friend's illness. Indeed, they themselves had practically forgotten it, thinking of it only as the overheard ravings of a sick man, not to be regarded as indicating mental unbalance since the man had regained his health.

Mr. Jones's first act on reaching New York had been to consult an eminent specialist in diseases of the brain, and have himself examined for insanity. The report was reassuring. Whatever he might have been in the past, this worthy physician declared him, to be now free from any taint of the disorder he so feared.

Jones went to the theater, danced, golfed and made brief cruises in the early spring, but an invitation to a flying meet was instantly and firmly declined. He never wished to see another aeroplane in his life. In fact, he did all that a man could to banish from his memory that dream which he had dreamed while cast upon the barren beach of an unnamed—absolutely an unnamed—rock in the Pacific.

If in visions of the night man-eating vegetables writhed their flaming tentacles, or strange yet familiar faces smiled or frowned upon him, he at least never spoke of the matter to any one.

So the three months had drifted by, and it was the latter end of March. One morning Jones slept later than usual—he never was an early riser—and when he sat up in bed, yawning, his window was a gray expanse against which sleet drove with a continual desolate rattling.

"Darn!" exclaimed Mr. Jones, at the end of his stretch. "Another day of 'indoor sports,' I see. How I hate a sleet storm! Philip!" he called.

Instantly his English man servant, an elderly but intensely efficient individual, appeared bearing coffee, newspapers, and the mail.

"You can get my bath ready. Now, let's see. Who's going to be married, and who desires the extreme boredom of my company—hello, I wonder what this can be—"

"This" was a small flat package, wrapped in white paper and addressed to himself in a small, perfect hand. Unlike a woman, he did not pause to contemplate its exterior, but untied the string immediately. Within the paper was a white pasteboard box, and inside that another box of Morocco leather, unquestionably a jewel case of some sort. He pressed the catch and it snapped open. What-in-the-world-

The whole room seemed to reel and sway about him dizzily. It vanished, and before him stretched a little glade all dark save where two white beams of light flashed and danced. Sergius—Miss Weston—the aeroplane—the flying monster! Was this some cruel joke that his friends had perpetrated against him.

For within the box, upon a bed of white velvet, rested an exquisite affair of gold, encrusted with blue-white diamonds. It was a tiny aeroplane, and enmeshed with it, its wings and the plane's interlocked, was a golden bat, with two tiny rubies for eyes.

Who had sent him this thing? Who had been so cruel as to taunt him with such a reminder of his time of madness? He raised box and jewel in his hand and was about to hurl it across the room when his eyes fell upon one of the letters scattered before him on the counterpane. The writing upon it was in that same small, yet distinctive hand that had appeared on the box-wrapping.

Dropping the leather case Jones hastily seized the letter and ripped it open. He, read:

MY DEAR FRIEND ROLAND:

"Two weeks ago I read in an old newspaper of your rescue and of your return to your native city. Until that moment I—we all—believed you to have been drowned in the sea, as was the enormous bat which carried you thither. We found its body washed up upon the shore, and believe me, my friend, I wept over it for sorrow at your loss and for such an end to such an heroic deed as yours.

"I know, however, that you must have been far more overcome by your terrible experience than the newspaper account indicated. You will not need to explain to me that otherwise you would have taken your yacht back to Joker Island and, if necessary, risked death in the cavern labyrinth seeking to return to aid me, if I needed aid. There are some friendships which spring into being without the need of years to build them up, and though few words were spoken, I know that ours was such a one."

"Well, the old son-of-a-gun," murmured Jones, "and he means it, too." The eyes he raised to Philip, coming to announce the readiness of the bath, were perceptibly wet, to that worthy Briton's great, though unrevealed, astonishment.

"Get out, Philip," was Jones's only reply. "I'll bath after a while."

Alone once more he eagerly resumed his reading:

"But enough of that. I am coming to New York soon—this is written from Tokio, where I have caused to be made a small remembrance which I am also mailing you—and then we can talk together.

"After you had so courageously and with incredible presence of mind flung yourself upon the great bat—"

Jones grinned, remembering the actual state of his feelings in that moment.

"—and been snatched away into the air, I managed to right the plane and we went on across the wall. I did not even know that you were gone. Miss Weston tried to tell me, but you know how great is the noise in flight. We came down upon the beach and I was overcome with dismay and self-reproach when I discovered that you were missing. I could perhaps have pursued the bat and rescued you from the sea, but then it was too late.

"Well, the yacht—the Monterey—was gone. I afterward learned that the traitorous and rascally Ivanovitch, believing that I had been killed or captured in the valley, and wishing to make off with the yacht which he afterward successfully sold, had deserted me early in the afternoon of the day you and I took flight.

"And, of course, Laroux and Martindale had to wait until the Monterey was gone before they looked up the island," muttered Jones.

"There was nothing else to be done, so I took Miss Weston back into the valley. We arrived there a little after sunrise and found things at the cave just as we had left them. I pulled away the rocks and we applied my restorative to my brother and the rest. They were considerably annoyed at my little strategy, but Paul was, I am sorry to say, so rejoiced over the desertion of my companions that he forgave me and persuaded the rest to do so.

"After making one flight in vain, I crossed the course of a tramp steamer and succeeded in dropping upon her deck a letter wrapped about a stone. It was fortunate that I succeeded, for there was barely sufficient petrol left to take me to land. The captain of the tramp, more I fear for the reward which the letter offered than for humanity, turned his vessel to the island and took us all off, together with our possessions.

"I have little more to tell you, save that in the month we spent in the valley Holloway, Haskins and I (Paul never cared for hunting) killed off most of the more dangerous animals. They are a peculiar collection. Over on the eastern side we discovered a cavern, or grotto, much bigger than any which Holloway had before explored. In it—it was, of course, daytime—we found scores of those enormous bats hanging, asleep.

"They are nothing but bats, although they are so big. They are fruit-eaters, subsisting upon the fruit of the palm-trees, something similar to a large date. I do not believe that it is their custom to attack other creatures, but, that they were simply actuated by curiosity. Still we thought it best to kill them, and their skins are really wonderful pieces of fur.

"Two of the best are for you and also the hide and head of the bear-creature you killed. We bagged two more of them, and I think they were the last of their kind.

"After we killed off the bats the death cabbages began to wither and decay, and now they, too, are all dead. It is evident that they lived almost entirely upon the bats, which they attracted by their palmlike crests. I do not think the bats could have had any sense of smell, though, do you?

"And now, I come to my conclusion to a very long letter. Mr. Holloway was mistaken in regard to the quantity of the substance, of which I told you, to be found in Joker Island. We were able to obtain altogether only about a pound of it, enough to make perhaps a million rubles' worth of what I told you it would make.

"This is not sufficient for the purpose of which I spoke, so, as both Paul and myself are fairly wealthy, we agreed to divide it among our companions. The largest share was received, of course, by Holloway. We gave him our portion as a wedding present. Did I tell you that Holloway and Miss Weston were married two weeks ago here in Tokio?"

For the love of Pete! Jones thought. First I thought it was Paul, and then I thought it was Sergius, only she didn't want him to know it, and all the while it was Holloway! I'll bet Miss Weston had Jim Haskins wondering if he wasn't the lucky one, too. Guess I was the only one not in the running. Well-

"They have, of course, my very kindest wishes for their happiness, but Paul—perhaps you knew of his hopes—he felt very badly. He has returned to Russia and is now fighting at the front, having, I fear purposely, obtained his transference to a very dangerous position. And why am I not at his side? Because, although those men with me proved traitors, such a thing would hardly turn me against the cause. And it is upon a mission for the cause that I am now about to engage, after visiting you in New York."

"Hurray!" ejaculated the reader. "Just wait until I introduce you to Messrs. Cocksure Martindale and Laroux! Oh, when will I forgive you two for the last three months?"

"It is a mission of some danger, perhaps, but also I think that it might interest a man of your adventurous disposition. I will tell you more of it later. Until that moment, my friend, believe me ever and always your friend and comrade of the past, perhaps—who knows?—of the future. "

SERGIUS ALEXIUS PETROFSKY

It was a long letter, but Mr. Jones read it through twice. Then he laid it down carefully, picked up the little box and stared at the golden bat and aeroplane with shining eyes and exultant face.

The sleet still beat upon the window, but it didn't bother Mr. Jones, for he was far away, on a little rock-walled island in the Pacific Ocean, which did have a name after all, and a most appropriate one—Joker Island!

Gertrude Barrows Bennett – A Short Biography

Gertrude Mabel Barrows was born in Minneapolis on 18th September 1884, to Charles, a Civil War veteran from Illinois, and Caroline Barrows (née Hatch).

Gertrude completed school up to the eighth grade, then switched to night school to study illustration. Although she had hopes of becoming an illustrator it was a goal she never achieved. As a fall back she began working as a stenographer, a career which she would keep to for the rest of her life.

But Gertrude had talent, writer's talent. Her first short story was written when she was just 17. Not you would think the usual subjects of curious teenage girls with headstrong ambitions but a science fiction story entitled 'The Curious Experience of Thomas Dunbar'. At the turn of the century magazines stands were full of cheap pulp magazines published weekly, fortnightly or monthly. She mailed the finished story to Argosy, then one of the top and most well known of the pulp magazines. The story was accepted and published in the March 1904 issue.

After this nothing seems to happen in her career as a writer for over a decade.

In 1909 Gertrude married the British journalist and explorer Stewart Bennett, and they moved to Philadelphia. A daughter was born the following year. Married life seemed blissful.

However tragedy now stepped in. Stewart died in a tropical storm while on a treasure hunting expedition.

Gertrude continued to work as a stenographer whilst trying to raise her new-born, and now fatherless, daughter.

Despite these pressures there is evidence that Gertrude began to write again. The obvious choice of interest continued to be ignored in favour of science fiction and with it a focus on dark fantasy.

Her mother, Caroline was an invalid and when Gertrude's father died she now also took on the care of her Mother.

During this time period Gertrude began to write a number of short stories, and then novels, in order to support her family. It was certainly the most productive part of her writing career.

Once Gertrude began to take care of her mother, she decided to return to fiction writing as a means of supporting her family. The first story she completed after her return to writing was the novella 'The Nightmare,' which appeared in All-Story Weekly in 1917. The story is set on an island separated from the rest of the world, on which evolution has taken a different course.

In submitting the story for publication Gertrude had requested that if it was accepted to be published then to use her pseudonym of Jean Vail. The Editor kindly agreed but under the pseudonym of Francis Stevens.

All-Story Weekly readers were pleased with the story as was Gertrude with her new name. She now wrote only under the moniker 'Francis Stevens'.

Over the next few years, Gertrude was rather more prolific than she had been. And her ideas were excellent and seemed also to influence others. (Indeed following the 'Nightmare' a year later was the similarly themed The Land That Time Forgot by Edgar Rice Burroughs).

Her short story "Friend Island" (All-Story Weekly, 1918), for example, is set in a 22nd-century ruled by women. Another story is the novella 'Serapion' (Argosy, 1920), about a man possessed by a supernatural creature.

In 1918 she published her first, and probably her best work the novel' The Citadel of Fear' (printed in several parts by Argosy, 1918). This lost world story focuses on a long-forgotten Aztec city, which is "rediscovered" during World War I.

A year later she published her only science fiction novel, 'The Heads of Cerberus' (The Thrill Book, 1919). One of the first dystopian novels, the book features a "grey dust from a silver phial" which transports anyone who inhales it to a totalitarian Philadelphia of 2118 AD

One of Bennett's most famous novels was 'Claimed!' (Argosy, 1920), in which a supernatural artefact summons an ancient and powerful god to early 20th century New Jersey. At the time it was said to be "one of the strangest and most compelling science fantasy novels you will ever read".

Her publisher at the time, The Thrill Book, had accepted several more of her stories for publication in the coming months. Her career was looking very promising. Sadly The Thrill Book failed only seven months after its first issue. Whatever stories it had stockpiled were lost.

Her Mother died in 1920 and once again Gertrude put her pen to one side.

In the mid-1920s, she moved to California. And for Gertrude her career was over. It was originally believed that she died in 1939 and for some years was estranged from her daughter. However recent new research has provided a death certificate stating that Gertrude Barrows Bennett died on February 2nd, 1948 at the age of 63 in San Francisco, California.

She did leave behind one mystery. For several decades her pseudonym Francis Stevens was believed to be that of the very popular Abraham Merritt. It was only finally revealed to be hers with the1952 book publication of 'Citadel of Fear'. Why no-one had spoken earlier to reveal this is not known.

In the ensuing years her work was barely printed but at the turn of the century a new interest and appetite had been shown for her works. Some have said she is the mother of 'Dark Fantasy' and her works had an influence both on Merritt and the dark master himself H.P. Lovecraft.

Gertrude Barrows Bennett - A Concise Bibliography

The Citadel of Fear (1918)
The Labyrinth (All-Story Weekly, July 27, August 3, and August 10, 1918)
The Heads of Cerberus (Thrill Book, 15 August 1919)
Avalon (Argosy, August 16 to September 6, 1919)
Claimed (Argosy, 1920)

Short Stories and Novellas

The Curious Experience of Thomas Dunbar (Argosy, March, 1904; as by G. M. Barrows)
The Nightmare, (All-Story Weekly, April 14, 1917)
Friend Island (All-Story Weekly, September 7, 1918)
Behind the Curtain (All-Story Weekly, September 21, 1918)
Unseen—Unfeared (People's Favorite Magazine Feb. 10, 1919)
The Elf-Trap (Argosy, July 5, 1919)
Serapion (Argosy Weekly, June 19, June 26, and July 3, 1920)
Sunfire (Weird Tales, July–August 1923, and September 1923)